Six Problems for Don Isidro Parodi

BY JORGE LUIS BORGES

Ficciones
Labyrinths
Dreamtigers
Other Inquisitions 1937–1952
A Personal Anthology
The Book of Imaginary Beings
The Aleph and Other Stories 1933–1969
Doctor Brodie's Report
Selected Poems 1923–1967
A Universal History of Infamy
In Praise of Darkness
Chronicles of Bustos Domecq
The Gold of the Tigers
The Book of Sand

BY ADOLFO BIOY-CASARES

The Invention of Morel and Other Stories
Diary of the War of the Pig
A Plan for Escape
Chronicles of Bustos Domecq
Asleep in the Sun

JORGE LUIS BORGES
ADOLFO BIOY-CASARES

Six Problems for Don Isidro Parodi

TRANSLATED BY
NORMAN THOMAS DI GIOVANNI

E. P. DUTTON
NEW YORK

Certain of these stories first appeared in the following periodicals:
American Poetry Review: "The God of the Bulls"
Antaeus: "The Twelve Figures of The World"
The Bennington Review: "Free Will and the Commendatore"
Salmagundi: "The Nights of Goliadkin"

The first three stories of this book have also been dramatized for radio broadcast by the BBC.

Published in the United States, 1981, by Elsevier-Dutton Publishing Co., Inc., 2 Park Avenue, New York, N.Y. 10016

Library of Congress Cataloging in Publication Data

Borges, Jorge Luis
    Six problems for Don Isidro Parodi.
    Translation of Seis problemas para don Isidro Parodi.
    CONTENTS: The twelve figures of the world.—The nights of Goliadkin.—The god of the bulls.—[etc.]
    I. Bioy Casares, Adolfo, joint author. II. Title.
PQ7797.B635S4413 1981   863   80-20107
ISBN: 0-525-48035-8

Published simultaneously in Canada by Clarke, Irwin & Company Limited, Toronto and Vancouver.

10 9 8 7 6 5 4 3 2 1

First Edition

Contents

Foreword

Good! It shall be. Revealment of myself!
But listen, for we must co-operate;
I don't drink tea: permit me the cigar!

ROBERT BROWNING

How fated, how interesting the idiosyncrasy of the *homme de lettres!* Literary Buenos Aires has probably not forgotten nor, I dare suggest, will ever forget my frank decision not to concede yet another preface to the claims—entirely legitimate, of course—of unimpeachable friendship and meritorious worth. We cannot but admit, however, that this Socratic "Bugsy"* is irresistible. What a peach of a man! With a peal of laughter that disarms me he acknowledges the perfect validity of my position; yet with an infectious chuckle, he repeats, persuasively and obstinately, that his book and our long-standing friendship demand my preface. Protestation is useless. *De guerre lasse,* I give in to sitting down at my trusty Remington, the partner and dumb confidant of so many of my flights into the blue.

Present-day pressures from the bank, the stock exchange, and the racetrack have been no impediment to my paying tribute—whether ensconced in the arm-

*Affectionate nickname for H. Bustos Domecq used among his intimates. [Footnote by H.B.D.]

7

chair of a Pullman car or as the skeptical patron of mud baths in more or less thermal spas—to the blood-curdling cruelties of the *roman policier.* Here I must risk confessing that I am no slave to fashion. Night after night in the central solitude of my bedroom the ingenious Sherlock Holmes retreats before the ever-fresh adventures of the wandering Ulysses, son of Laertes and seed of Zeus. But the admirer of the stern Mediterranean epic sips in many gardens. Bolstered by the French sleuth M. Lecoq, I have turned over dusty dossiers; I have pricked up my ears in vast imaginary country houses so as to capture the muffled footsteps of the gentleman-*cambrioleur;* in the grim wastes of Dartmoor, enclosed in an English fog, the great luminous hound has devoured me. To continue would be in bad taste. The reader knows my credentials. I too have been in Boeotia.

Before embarking on a fruitful analysis of the basic elements of this *recueil,* I beg the reader's leave to congratulate myself that at last in the motley Musée Grevin of *belles lettres . . . criminologiques* an Argentine hero has made his appearance in a purely Argentine setting. What an uncommon pleasure it is—between puffs of the aromatic herb and with an unmistakable First Empire cognac at one's elbow—to savor a detective story which does not obey the rigid rules of a foreign, Anglo-Saxon market and which I have no hesitation in putting on the same level as those authors recommended to keen London enthusiasts by the incorruptible Crime Club! Let me also modestly point out my satisfaction as a native of Buenos Aires in learning that our writer, although from the provinces, has proved himself deaf to the call of narrow parochialism and has had the sense to choose Buenos Aires as the natural frame for his etchings of local scenes.

Nor shall I fail to applaud the courage and good taste shown by our much-loved "Bugsy"* in turning his back on the dark and dissolute fat-man stereotype from Rosario. However, two elements are missing from this metropolitan palette, and I venture to demand them of future books. They are our silky, feminine Florida Street in sublime procession before the avid eyes of its shop windows; and the melancholy quarter of La Boca, slumbering by the docks, when the last street-corner bar has shut its metal eyelids, and an accordion, unvanquished in the dark, greets the now paling constellations.

At this point let us frame the most salient and at the same time most profound feature of the author of *Six Problems for Don Isidro Parodi*. I have mentioned—let there be no mistake—concision, the art of *brûler les étapes*. H. Bustos Domecq is at all times an attentive servant of his public. In his stories there are no false trails or confusing timetables. He spares us all blind alleys. Offspring of the tradition of the tragic Edgar Allan Poe, the mandarin M. P. Shiel, and Baroness Orczy, our author concentrates on the main events in his cases—the statement of the problem and its illuminating solution. Mere puppets of curiosity—if not under direct pressure from the police—the characters gather in a colorful flock in the now legendary cell 273. On their first visit they put forward the mystery that troubles them; on their second they hear its solution, which astounds young and old alike. The author, whose skill is as compact as it is artistic, reduces elementary reality and heaps all the laurels of the case on the brow of Parodi alone. The less perceptive reader will smile, suspecting the deliberate omission of some

*See footnote on p. 7. [Footnote by H.B.D.]

tedious inquiry and the unintentional omission of more than one inspired insight made by a gentleman on whose identity it would be inappropriate to dwell.

Let us look closely at the book. It consists of six stories. I obviously cannot hide my penchant for "Tadeo Limardo's Victim," a story of Slavonic inspiration, which combines a thrilling plot with a probe into more than one aspect of morbid Dostoevskian psychology. And it does this while still charming us with a revelation of a sui generis world that lies on the fringe of our European veneer and refined egocentricity. I also recall with pleasure "Tai An's Long Search," which is a new and original treatment of the classic problem of the hidden object. Poe began it with "The Purloined Letter"; Lynn Brock attempts a Parisian variation with *The Two of Diamonds,* an elegantly written piece spoiled by a stuffed dog; Carter Dickson, less successfully, falls back on a central heating system radiator. It would be unjust, to say the least, not to mention "Free Will and the Commendatore," a puzzle whose impeccable solution will—*parole de gentilhomme* —bewilder even the most perceptive reader.

One of the tasks which test the mettle of a first-class writer must surely be skillful, elegant characterization. The unsophisticated Neapolitan puppeteer who once brought fantasy to our childhood Sundays solved the problem in a makeshift way. He gave Punch a hunchback, Pierrot a starched collar, Columbine the naughtiest smile in the world, and Harlequin a harlequin suit. Mutatis mutandis, H. Bustos Domecq operates in a similar way. In short, he resorts to the heavy strokes of the caricaturist, although when drawn by his jovial pen the inevitable exaggerations typical of the genre have little to do with the physical traits of his puppets; instead, he breathes life into them by dwelling on their habits of speech. In return for a certain abuse of the good salt of our native cooking, the irrepressible satirist presents us with an entire portrait gallery of our day. In it we find the religious grande dame with her strong sensibility; the journalist with his sharp pencil who, with more ease than elegance, churns out all manner of articles; the decidedly amiable playboy from a well-to-do family, a rake who keeps late hours and is easily recognizable by his slicked-back hair and inevitable polo ponies; the soft-spoken, courteous Chinese of old literary convention, whom I look on as a pastiche of the art of rhetoric rather than as a living person; and the gentleman, artist and lover, interested alike in feasts of the mind and flesh, in the learned tomes of the Jockey Club Library, and in the *piste* of the same establishment's fencing competitions. One touch forecasts the gloomiest of sociological developments. From this fresco of what I do not hesitate to call "contemporary Argentina" is missing the silhouette of the gaucho on horseback, and in his place stands—and I expose the phenomenon in all its repulsive crudeness—the Jew, the Israelite. The debonair figure of the hoodlum of our city's outer slums suffers a similar *capitis diminutio.* This robust half-breed who in bygone days stole the scene with his lascivious steps on the dance floor at Hansen's, where only the uppercut curbed the knife, is now called Tulio Savastano, and he fritters away his by no means common talents in the most inane gossip. We are barely rescued from this wearisome laxity by Pardo Salivazo, a peripheral but lively character who is another proof of the stylistic qualities of H. Bustos.

But all is not flowers. The Attic censor in me condemns without appeal the tiring extravagance of colorful but episodic brush strokes—an overgrown thicket that clutters and obscures the Parthenon's sharp outline.

The pen which in our satirist's hand becomes a scalpel is soon blunted when it works on the living flesh of don Isidro Parodi. For our amusement the author introduces the most priceless of old-time Argentines, a portrait that now takes its place beside those equally famous ones bequeathed us by Del Campo, Hernández, and other high priests of our traditional guitar, among whom towers the author of *Martín Fierro.*

In the stirring annals of criminal investigation, the honor of being the first detective to be a jailbird goes to don Isidro. Any critic with a sound nose can, however, point to several possible derivatives. Without leaving his nightly den in the Faubourg St. Germain, the gentleman Auguste Dupin captures the troublesome ape who caused the tragedies in the Rue Morgue; Prince Zaleski, from his remote palace retreat, where in sumptuous surroundings the jewel rubs shoulders with the music box, the amphora with the sarcophagus, the idol with the winged bull, solves the crimes of London; and last but not least, Max Carrados carries with him everywhere the portable jail cell of his blindness. Such sedentary sleuths, such strange *voyageurs autour de la chambre,* are, if only in part, forerunners of our Parodi. Perhaps an inevitable character in the development of detective fiction, Parodi's appearance, his *trouvaille,* is an Argentine achievement, produced—it should be noted—during the presidency of Dr. Castillo. Parodi's lack of mobility is the symbol and epitome of intellectuality, and it stands as a challenge to the pointless, frenetic action of American detective stories, which an overcritical yet quite accurate mind might compare with the celebrated squirrel of legend.

But I think I notice a veiled impatience in my reader's face. Nowadays, interest in adventure ranks above philosophical dialogue. The time has come to say goodbye. To this point we have walked together; from here, face to face with the book, you are on your own.

Gervasio Montenegro
Member, Argentine Academy
of Letters

Buenos Aires,
November 20, 1942

Six
Problems
for Don Isidro
Parodi

The Twelve Figures of the World

To the memory of José S. Álvarez

I

Capricorn, Aquarius, Pisces, Aries, Taurus, thought Achilles Molinari in his sleep. Then came a moment of uncertainty. He saw the Scales, the Scorpion. Realizing his mistake, he woke with a start.

The sun had warmed his face. On the night table, perched atop a copy of the *Bristol Almanac* and a handful of lottery tickets, his alarm clock showed twenty to ten. Still reciting the signs, Molinari got up. He looked out of the window. There on the street corner stood the unknown man.

Molinari smiled knowingly. Ambling down the corridor, he returned with his razor, a brush, a sliver of yellow soap, and a cup of steaming water. He flung the window open wide, stared down at the unknown man with exaggerated calm, and slowly, whistling the tango "Marked Card," began to shave.

Ten minutes later Molinari was on the street, wearing his brown suit on which he still owed the Rabuffi chain of Great English Tailor Shops the final two payments. He strolled to the corner. At once, the man became absorbed in the posted lottery results.

Molinari, accustomed by now to this dreary pretense, went on to the corner of Humberto I. A bus pulled up; he boarded it. To make it easier for the man tailing him, Molinari sat at the front. Two or three blocks farther on, he glanced around. The unknown man, easily recognizable by his dark glasses, was reading a newspaper. Before reaching downtown, the bus had filled up. Molinari could have gotten off without being detected, but he had a better plan. He stayed on until the Palermo Beer Gardens. There, never once looking back, he made his way north, skirting the penitentiary wall, and entered the front gate. He thought he was behaving normally, but before reaching the armed guards he threw away a cigarette that he had just lit. He spoke briefly to a man in shirtsleeves behind a counter. A prison officer accompanied him to cell 273.

Fourteen years earlier, Agustín R. Bonorino, the butcher, while taking part in a carnival parade in Belgrano rigged out as an Italian, received a fatal conk on the head. It was common knowledge that the seltzer bottle that had laid him low had been wielded by one of the goons in the gang known as the Holy Hoofs. But since the Holies were useful during elections, the police decided that the culprit was Isidro Parodi, who some claimed was an anarchist, by which they meant an oddball. Actually, Isidro Parodi was neither. He owned a barbershop in Barracas, on the Southside of Buenos Aires, and he had been unwise enough to have let a room to a police clerk from the Eighth Precinct, who owed him a year's back rent. This conjunction of adverse circumstances had sealed Parodi's fate. The evidence of witnesses (all of whom belonged to the Holy Hoofs) was unanimous; Parodi was sentenced to twenty-one years. A sedentary life had worked a change in the homicide of 1919; he was now in his forties, sententious and fat, and had a shaved head and unusually wise eyes. These eyes were now fixed on young Molinari.

"What can I do for you, my friend?"

The tone was not overly cordial, but Molinari knew that Parodi was not averse to visits. Besides, any reaction of Parodi's was less important than Molinari's need to find a confidant and a counselor. Slowly and efficiently, Parodi brewed maté in a small blue mug. He offered some to Molinari. Molinari, though impatient to explain the irreversible adventure that had turned his life upside down, knew it was pointless to try to hurry Isidro Parodi. Molinari astounded himself by the ease with which he launched into a casual discussion of the racetrack and how it was rigged nowadays so that nobody could tell who was going to win anymore. Don Isidro paid no attention. Taking up his favorite gripe, he railed on and on against the Italians, who had wormed their way into everything—not excluding the state penitentiary.

"Now it's full of foreigners of the most dubious pedigree," he said, "and nobody knows where they come from."

Molinari, who was prone to nationalistic sentiments, joined battle to say that he was fed up with Italians and Druses, not to mention English capitalists, who had filled Argentina with railways and meat-packing plants. Only yesterday he'd walked into the All-Star Pizza Parlor, and the first thing he set eyes on was an Italian.

"Tell me," said don Isidro, "this Italian that's on your mind—is it a man or a woman?"

"Neither," replied Molinari, to the point. "Don Isidro, I have killed a man."

"They say I killed one too, and yet look at me. Take

it easy. This business of the Druses is complicated, but as long as no clerk in the Eighth Precinct has it in for you, maybe your hide can be saved."

Molinari was taken aback. Then he remembered that his name had been linked to the mystery of Ibn Khaldun's villa by an unscrupulous newspaper—a newspaper that was a breed apart from the dynamic daily for which Molinari reported on soccer as well as the nobler sports. He recalled that Parodi kept his mind sharp and, thanks to his astuteness and the generous oversight of Assistant Chief Grondona, always submitted the afternoon papers to intelligent scrutiny. In fact, don Isidro was not unaware of the recent demise of Ibn Khaldun. Nonetheless, he asked Molinari to explain what had happened, requesting him not to speak fast, since he was becoming a bit hard of hearing. Molinari, almost relaxed, told this story:

"Believe me, I'm a modern guy, a man of my times. I've seen a thing or two, but I also enjoy a bit of meditation. It seems to me that mankind has gone beyond the stage of materialism. Holy Communion and the mobs who attended the recent Eucharistic Congress left me with something unforgettable. As you said last time—and believe you me, your words didn't fall on deaf ears—life's enigma has to be solved. Look, fakirs and yogis, with their breathing exercises and their gimmicks, know a thing or two. As a good Catholic, I've renounced the Honor and Patria Spiritualist Institute, but I'm convinced that the Druses form a forward-looking community and are closer to the mystery than many who go to Mass every Sunday. For instance, Dr. Ibn Khaldun had a real showplace out in Villa Mazzini, with a fabulous library. I first met him at Radio Phoenix on Arbor Day. He made a really meaningful speech, and he praised me for an article of mine that someone had sent him. He took me to his house, lent me serious books, and invited me to a party he was giving. The female element was missing, but these cultural exchanges are something, let me tell you. People accuse the Druses of believing in idols, but in their assembly room there's a metal statue of a bull that must be worth a king's ransom. Every Friday the Akils—they're the initiates—gather around the bull. A while ago, Dr. Ibn Khaldun wanted me to be initiated. I didn't see how I could refuse; I wanted to be on good terms with the old guy, and man doesn't live by bread alone. The Druses are a closed group; some of them didn't think a Westerner was worthy of entering the brotherhood. To give one example, Abdul Hassam, the owner of a fleet of trucks that carry frozen meat, recalled that the number of the chosen is fixed and that it's not in the bylaws to make converts. The treasurer, Izz-al-Din, was opposed too. But he's a nobody who spends his whole day at a desk scribbling figures in a ledger. Dr. Ibn Khaldun laughed off him and his books. Still, these reactionaries, with their outdated prejudices, kept trying to cut the ground from under me, and I wouldn't hesitate to come right out and say that indirectly they're to blame for everything. The eleventh of August I had a letter from Ibn Khaldun, informing me that on the fourteenth I'd be put through a pretty stiff test, for which I had to prepare myself."

"And what did you have to do to prepare yourself?" asked Parodi.

"Well, as I'm sure you know, three days on nothing but tea, learning the signs of the Zodiac—in their correct order—the way they appear in the *Bristol Almanac.* I asked for sick leave at the Sanitation Department, where I work mornings. At first, it surprised me that the ceremony was to take place on a Sunday and not on a Friday, but the letter explained that for an examination as important as this one the Lord's day was more appropriate. I was told to turn up at the villa before midnight. All Friday and Saturday I was relatively calm, but on Sunday I woke up with a bad case of nerves. You see, don Isidro, now that I think about it I'm sure I already had a premonition of what was going to happen. But I didn't cave in. I spent the whole day with the book in my hand. It was comical. Every five minutes I looked at my watch to see if I could have another glass of tea. I don't know why the watch; I had to drink anyway. My throat was parched, and it cried out for liquid. And then, although I had been waiting and waiting for the hour of the examination, I went and missed the train out of Retiro. The one I took, the eleven-eighteen, was slower than the one I should have been on.

"Despite being well rehearsed, I kept studying the *Almanac* on the train. I was annoyed by a gang of idiots arguing about how the Millionaires trounced the Chacarita Juniors and, believe you me, they didn't know a thing about soccer. I got off at Belgrano R. The villa's located about thirteen blocks from the station. I thought the walk was going to refresh me; instead, it left me bushed. Following Ibn Khaldun's instructions to the letter, I phoned him from the bar at the corner of Rosetti Street.

"In front of the villa was a line of parked cars; the house was lit up as if for a wake, and from a long way off you could hear the sound of voices. Ibn Khaldun was waiting for me in the doorway. It struck me that he had aged. I'd always seen him by day; only that night did I realize that with his beard and all he looked a bit like D'Annunzio. Here's one of life's little ironies.

Worried half out of my wits over the examination, I go and notice a foolish thing like that. We made our way along the brick walk that went around the house and entered by a back door. Izz-al-Din was in the office, standing beside the files."

"It's fourteen years now that I've been filed away," remarked don Isidro sweetly. "But this office—describe the place a little."

"Well, it's very simple. The office is on the upper floor. A stairway comes down directly into the assembly room. That's where the Druses were, about a hundred and fifty of them, all veiled and dressed in white robes, standing around the metal bull. The files are in an alcove off the office; it's an inner room. I've always maintained that in the long run a room without a proper window is unhealthy. You feel the same, don't you?"

"Don't talk to me about rooms without windows. Since settling here on the Northside I'm fed up with blank walls. Describe the office."

"It's a big room. There's an oak desk with an Olivetti on it, some really comfortable armchairs that you sink down to your ears in, one of those Turkish pipe things that seemed to be broken but still worth a mint, a crystal chandelier, a kind of futuristic-looking Oriental carpet, a bust of Napoleon, a library of serious books—César Cantú's *World History, The Wonders of the World and of Man, The International Library of Famous Authors,* the *Daily Mirror Yearbook,* Peluffo's *Illustrated Gardener, The Treasure of Youth,* Lombroso's *Criminal Woman,* and who knows what else.

"Izz-al-Din was nervous. Right away I found out why; he'd gone back to work on his books. There was an enormous stack of them on the table. Dr. Ibn Khaldun, concerned about my examination, wanted to get rid of Izz-al-Din and he said to him, 'Don't worry. I'll look into your books later tonight.'

"I don't know whether Izz-al-Din believed him or not. He left to put on his robe to go down with the others. He never once glanced at me. As soon as we were alone, Dr. Ibn Khaldun said to me, 'Have you fasted faithfully? Have you learned the twelve figures of the world?'

"I assured him that since ten o'clock on Thursday night—earlier that evening, in the company of some drumbeaters for the new sensibility, I had eaten a light stew and some roast beef at the Wholesale Market—I'd had nothing but plain tea.

"Then Ibn Khaldun asked me to recite the names of the twelve figures. I recited them without a single mistake; he made me repeat the list five or six times. Finally, he said to me, 'I see you've carried out your instructions. This wouldn't have been enough, however, had you not been diligent and brave. I know that you are, and I've decided to ignore your detractors. I shall put you to a single test—the most perilous and difficult of all. Thirty years ago, in the mountains of Lebanon, I myself performed it, but my masters assigned me other easier tests beforehand. I found a coin at the bottom of the sea, a forest made of air, a chalice at the center of the earth, a saber condemned to Hell. You will not seek four magical objects; you shall seek out the four masters who make up the veiled tetragon of the Godhead. Right now, entrusted with a pious mission, they are gathered around the metal bull, praying with their brothers, the Akils, who are also veiled. No mark distinguishes them, but your heart will recognize them. I command you to bring Yusuf. You will descend to the auditorium, remembering in their exact order the twelve figures of the heavens. When you reach the last figure, the sign of Pisces, you shall return to the first, which is Aries, and so on in rotation. Thrice you will weave a circle round the Akils and your steps will lead you to Yusuf—so long as you have not changed the order of the figures. You will tell him, "Ibn Khaldun summons," and you will bring him here. Then I shall command you to bring the second master, then the third, then the fourth.'

"Luckily, reading and rereading the *Bristol Almanac* so many times had engraved the twelve figures in my mind; but to make a mistake all you need is to be told not to. I was not daunted, I assure you, but I had a premonition. Ibn Khaldun shook my hand, told me his prayers would be with me, and I started down the stairs into the gathering. I was very busy with the figures; as if that weren't enough, those white backs, those bowed heads, those smooth masks, and that sacred bull I'd never before seen close up made me uneasy. Still, I circled three times without a mistake, and I found myself behind a person in a sheet who looked to me exactly like all the others. But as my mind was working on the signs of the Zodiac, I had no time to think, and I said, 'Ibn Khaldun summons.' The man followed me. I kept the signs in mind as we climbed the stairway and entered the office. Ibn Khaldun was praying; he made Yusuf enter the alcove, and almost immediately he turned again and said to me, 'Now bring Ibrahim.' I went back to the assembly, made my three turns, stopped behind another man in a sheet, and said, 'Ibn Khaldun summons.' Leading him, I returned to the office."

"Whoa, my friend, whoa," said Parodi. "Are you sure that while you were weaving your three circles no one left the office?"

"Look, I can tell you positively. I admit I was concentrating on the figures and all that, but I'm not that foolish. I didn't take my eyes off that door. Nobody went in or came out.

"Ibn Khaldun took Ibrahim by the arm and ushered him into the other room. Then he said to me, 'Now bring Izz-al-Din.' A strange thing, don Isidro, the first two times I had all the confidence in the world; this time I lost my nerve. I went down, I walked around the Druses three times, and I returned with Izz-al-Din. I was absolutely exhausted. On the stairway my sight blurred. I figured it was my kidneys acting up. Everything seemed different—even the man beside me. Ibn Khaldun himself had so much faith in me by now that I found him playing a game of solitaire instead of praying. He herded Izz-al-Din into the alcove and, speaking like a father, said to me, 'This exercise has worn you out. I shall seek the fourth initiate—Kahlil.'

"Fatigue is the enemy of concentration, but as soon as Ibn Khaldun went out, I put my nose to the gallery railing and spied on him. He made his three turns without any ado, took Kahlil by the arm, and brought him back up. I said that the alcove had no other door than the one that opened into the office. Well, Ibn Khaldun entered that door with Kahlil; straightaway he came out with the four veiled Druses. He made the sign of the cross, because these Druses are very devout people. Then he told them in good Argentine to take off their veils. You'll say I've made all this up, but there was Izz-al-Din with that foreign face of his, and Kahlil, the assistant manager of Dyno-Rod Pipe, Drain, and Hygiene Services, and Yusuf, the brother-in-law of a man who talks through his nose, and Ibrahim, Ibn Khaldun's partner, unshaven and white as a corpse. A hundred and fifty identical Druses, and here were the four masters!

"Dr. Ibn Khaldun almost embraced me. But the others were the sort that hate to show their feelings, and being full of superstitions and taboos they wouldn't let him twist their arms. They got angry with him in Druse. Poor Ibn Khaldun tried hard to convince them, but in the end he had to submit. He said he would put me to another test, an extremely difficult one this time, but that in this test the lives of all of them and maybe the fate of the world would be at stake.

" 'We'll blindfold you with this veil,' he said. 'We'll put this long rod in your hand, and each of us will hide in some corner or other of the house or garden. You'll wait here until the clock strikes twelve. Then you'll search for us, one by one, guided by the figures. These signs rule the world. While the examination lasts, we shall entrust you with the order of the figures. The entire cosmos will be in your power. If you do not change the order of the Zodiac, our fate and the fate of the world will continue on their predetermined course. If you make a mistake—if, for instance, after Libra you come up with Leo or Scorpio—the master you seek will perish, and the whole wide world will fall victim to the menace of wind and water and fire.'

"Everyone agreed, except for Izz-al-Din. He'd stuffed himself with so much salami that his eyes were half shut, and he was so flustered that on leaving he shook hands with us all, one by one—a thing he never does.

"They handed me a bamboo rod, blindfolded me, and scattered. I was alone. I was petrified! I had to imagine the figures without changing their order; I had to wait for the stroke of twelve, which I was sure would never come, knowing all the while that I'd have to find my way through that house. Suddenly the place seemed not only interminable but completely unfamiliar. Without trying to, I kept thinking about the stairway, the landings, the furniture I'd bump into, the cellars, the courtyard, the skylights. And I heard all sorts of things—the branches of the trees in the garden; some footsteps upstairs; the Druses, who were leaving the house; Abd-al-Malik's Isotta starting up. You know, he's the one who won the Raggio Olive Oil raffle. Well, everybody was leaving and there I was, all alone in the mansion, with those Druses hiding God knows where. When midnight struck I nearly jumped out of my skin! I set out with my wand—me, a young man, still in the prime of life—walking like a cripple, like a blind man, if you know what I mean. I immediately turned left. The brother-in-law of the guy that talks through his nose has a lot of savoir faire, and I thought I'd find him under the table. All this time, clear as a bell, I saw Libra, Scorpio, Sagittarius, and all those illustrations. I forgot the first landing and kept stumbling. Then I entered the conservatory. Suddenly I was lost. I couldn't find either the door or the walls. What else would you expect after three days on plain tea, not to mention the strain of concentration? Still, I took myself in hand and headed for the dumbwaiter, suspecting that one of them might have hidden himself in the coalbin. But these Druses, no matter how educated they are, haven't our native Argentine cunning. I went back to the assembly room. I tripped over a three-legged table used by some of the Druses who still believe in spiritualism—as if they were back in the Middle Ages. I felt that all the eyes in the oil paintings were staring at me. You'll probably laugh—my younger sister always said I have something of the mad poet in me. But I was on my toes, and at once I discovered Ibn Khaldun. I stretched out an arm and there he was. Without much trouble we found the stairway, which turned out to be a lot closer than I thought, and we entered the office. On our way, we didn't exchange a single word. I was too busy concentrating on the signs. I left him and went to look for another Druse. Just then I heard a stifled laugh. For the first time, a doubt crossed my mind. I began to think they were laughing at me. Suddenly I heard a cry. I'd swear I made no mistake with the signs. But what with my anger and then my surprise I may have mixed them up—I never try to hide the truth. I turned around and, prodding with my rod, I went back into the office. I tripped over something on the floor. I squatted down. My hand touched hair; I felt a nose, eyes. Without realizing what I was doing, I tore off the blindfold.

"Ibn Khaldun lay on the floor, his mouth covered with saliva and blood. I touched him; he was still warm but he was already a corpse. There was no one in the room. I saw the rod, which had fallen from my hand. Blood stained the tip of it. Only then did I see I had killed him. When I heard the laugh and the cry, I must have become momentarily confused and changed the order of the figures. That cost a man his life—maybe even the lives of the four masters. I looked over the gallery and called out. Nobody answered. In a panic, I ran through the back part of the house, mumbling to myself, 'The Ram, the Bull, the Twins,' trying to keep the world in one piece. Despite the fact that the grounds were nearly a block long, I was at the garden wall in no time. Tullido Ferrarotti always said I had a future in the middle-distance events, but that night I turned into a champion high-jumper. With one leap I cleared the wall, which is close to six feet high. Picking myself up from the ditch and brushing off the pieces of broken glass that clung to me, I found I was coughing. From the villa poured a column of smoke, thick and black as mattress stuffing. Out of condition or not, I sprinted like I used to in the old days. When I reached Rosetti Street I turned around. The sky was lit up like Independence Day. The house was burning —that's what a mix-up in the figures could do! Just the thought of it made my mouth drier than a parrot's tongue. Catching a glimpse of a cop on the corner, I did an about-face, then dashed across some open lots. What a disgrace that we still have them in this city! As a good Argentine it hurt me, let me tell you, and what with shaking off a pack of dogs I was quite dizzy. All it takes is one to start barking for all the others to deafen you. Out there in those Westside neighborhoods you're not safe walking around, and there's no police of any kind. But after a while, seeing I was on Charlone Street, I calmed down. A right, then a left, and I found myself at the wall of the Chacarita. A bunch of hooligans standing on a street corner began chanting, 'The Ram, the Bull,' and making noises unfit for a human mouth. What could I do? I gave them a wide berth. Would you believe it took some time before I realized I was repeating the names of the signs out loud? I lost my way again. You know how it is out in that part of the city. They don't know a thing about urbanization, and all the streets end up in a labyrinth. The idea of looking for transportation didn't even occur to me. My shoes were a mess. I got home just about the time the trash men were making their rounds. I was sick with exhaustion; I think I was even running a temperature. I threw myself down on my bed, but so as not to lose my concentration on the figures I wouldn't let myself fall asleep.

"At noon I asked for sick leave from both the newspaper and the Sanitation Department. That was when my neighbor poked his head in—he's on the road for Brylcreem—and he insisted on taking me to his room for a spaghetti feed. I'm opening my heart to you now. At first I felt a little better. My friend has a bit of the old savoir faire, and he uncorked a nice little local muscatel. But I was in no mood for deep conversation. Using the excuse that the sauce sat on my stomach like lead, I retired to my room. I didn't go out all day. Still, not being a hermit and worried stiff about what had happened the night before, I asked the landlady to bring me a copy of the afternoon paper. I skipped the sports page, plunged straight into the crime news, and saw the photographs of the holocaust. At twelve-thirty in the morning a fire of vast proportions had broken out in the Villa Mazzini home of Dr. Ibn Khaldun. Despite the brave efforts of the Fire Department, the property was gutted by the flames, its owner, the distinguished member of the Syrio-Lebanese community, also perishing in the blaze. Dr. Ibn Khaldun was a pioneer in the importation of linoleum substitutes. I was horror-stricken. Baudizzone, who's always sloppy in his reporting, had made several errors. For example, he completely overlooked the religious ceremony and said that that night they had met to read the minutes and to reelect officers. A little before the disaster, the Messrs. Kahlil, Yusuf, and Ibrahim had left the premises. They claimed that up until midnight they had been engaged in amicable conversation with the deceased, who, far from foreseeing the tragedy that would put an end to his days and would reduce to ashes a residence characteristic of our city's western zone, displayed his usual esprit. The cause of the great conflagration was still to be determined.

"I'm not afraid of work, but from then on I haven't

been back to the paper or to the department. I've been in a terrible state. Two days later, I was paid a visit by an affable gentleman, who questioned me about my part in the requisition of brooms and mops for the personnel canteen at the government warehouse on Bucarelli Street. Then he changed the subject and spoke of foreign communities, and he was especially interested in the Syrio-Lebanese. He vaguely promised to come back again, but he never did. Instead, a total stranger installed himself on my street corner, and he follows me everywhere, hiding behind dark glasses. I know you aren't a man to be taken in by the police or by anybody else. Help me, don Isidro. I'm desperate!"

"I'm neither a wizard nor a magician—I don't go around solving riddles. I won't deny you a helping hand, however. But there's one condition. Promise me you'll do everything I tell you."

"Whatever you say, don Isidro."

"Good. We'll begin right now. Recite in order the figures of the *Almanac.*"

"Aries, Taurus, Gemini, Cancer, Leo, Virgo, Libra, Scorpio, Sagittarius, Capricorn, Aquarius, Pisces."

"Fine. Now say them backward."

Molinari, his face pale, mumbled, "Riesa, Rustau—"

"Can the pig Latin. Now change the order and say the figures any way you like."

"Change the order? You haven't understood me, don Isidro. That can't be done!"

"No? Give the first sign, the last, and next to last."

On the brink of terror, Molinari obeyed. Then he looked wildly around him.

"Good. Now that you've emptied your head of this nonsense, off you go to the paper. And don't worry about a thing."

Speechless, redeemed, dumbfounded, Molinari left the jail. Outside, the man was waiting for him.

II

A week later, Molinari told himself that he couldn't wait any longer, he'd have to pay a second visit to the penitentiary. Still, having to face Parodi troubled him, for Parodi had seen through his vanity and his pitiful gullibility. It galled him that a man of his sophistication should let himself be bamboozled by a pack of foreign fanatics! At the same time, the appearances of the affable gentleman had become more frequent and more sinister. He spoke not only of the Syrio-Lebanese but also of the Druses of Lebanon. And his conversation was enriched by new subjects—for example, the abolition of torture in 1813, the merits of an electric prod recently imported from Bremen by the Criminal Investigation Division, and so forth.

One rainy morning, Molinari caught the bus at the corner of Humberto I. When he got off in Palermo, the unknown man got off too. He had graduated from dark glasses to a blond beard.

As usual, Parodi received Molinari with a certain curtness. The older man had the tact not to refer to the Villa Mazzini mystery. He launched into a theme that was almost obsessive with him—what a man could do with a solid knowledge of cards. He called to mind the teachings of Lynxie Rivarola, who was hit by a chair and died just as he drew a second ace of spades from a special device he had up his sleeve. Complementing the anecdote, Parodi brought out a greasy pack of cards, had Molinari shuffle them, and asked him to lay out the cards, face down.

"My dear friend," said Parodi, "you who have magic powers are going to hand this poor old man the four of hearts."

"I've—I've never pretended to have magic powers," stammered Molinari. "You know very well, sir, that I've cut all ties with those fanatics."

"You've cut that deck too. Give me the four of hearts. Don't be afraid. It's the first card you'll reach for."

His hand shaking, Molinari picked up a card at random and gave it to Parodi.

"Wonderful," Parodi said, glancing at it. "Now you're going to give me the jack of spades."

Molinari picked another card and handed it over.

"Now the seven of clubs."

Molinari handed Parodi a card.

"The exercise has tired you. I'll pick the last card for you. It's the king of hearts."

Casually, Parodi drew a card and added it to the three previous ones. Then he told Molinari to turn them up. They were the king of hearts, the seven of clubs, the jack of spades, and the four of hearts.

"Don't be so amazed," said Parodi. "Among these cards is one that's marked—the first I asked for, but not the first you gave me. I asked for the four of hearts; you gave me the jack of spades. I asked for the jack of spades; you gave me the seven of clubs. I asked for the seven of clubs; you gave me the king of hearts. Then I said you were tired and that I would pick the fourth card myself—the king of hearts. I picked the four of hearts, the marked card.

"Ibn Khaldun did the same. He ordered you to seek out Druse number one, and you brought him number two. He asked for number two, and you brought him three. He asked for three and you brought him four. He told you he'd find number four himself, and he brought number one. Number one was Ibrahim, his closest friend. Ibn Khaldun had no trouble recognizing him even among the crowd. You see—this is what happens to people who get themselves mixed up with foreigners. You told me yourself that the Druses are a closed society. You were right, and the most closed of them all was Ibn Khaldun, the dean of the community. The rest were satisfied just to make fun of a native Argentine; it was Ibn Khaldun who wanted to rub it in. He told you to appear on a Sunday, and you said yourself that Friday was the day of his services. To give you a case of nerves he put you on a three-day diet of tea and the *Bristol Almanac.* On top of that, he made you walk I don't know how many blocks. He plunged you into the midst of a gathering of Druses who were got up in bedsheets and, as if you needed more confusing, he made up the business of the figures of the *Almanac.* The man was having his fun. He hadn't yet looked over Izz-al-Din's account books—nor would he ever. Those were the books they were talking about when you entered. You thought they were speaking about mere novels and poetry. Who knows what fiddling the treasurer had done. But what's certain is that he killed Ibn Khaldun and burned down the house so that no one would ever see those books. He said goodbye to you all, he shook hands—a thing he never did—to make you think he had left. He hid nearby, waited for the others to leave—by then they'd have had enough of the joke—and when you, with the rod and blindfold, were looking for Ibn Khaldun, Izz-al-Din went back to the office. When you returned with the old man, the two of them laughed to see you walking around like a blind man. You went out to find a second Druse. Ibn Khaldun followed you so that you would find him again; you made four trips, bumping into things and bringing the same person back each time. The treasurer then knifed him in the back; you heard the cry. While you were going back to the room, feeling your way, Izz-al-Din fled, setting fire to the books. After that, to justify the disappearance of the books, he set fire to the house."

Pujato, Province of Santa Fe,
December 27, 1941

The Nights
of Goliadkin

To the memory of the Repentant Thief

I

Tall, distinguished, bland, his profile romantic, his
brush mustache tinted, Gervasio Montenegro stepped
with blasé elegance into the police van and let himself
be chauffeured to the penitentiary. He found himself
in a paradoxical situation. The countless readers of
evening papers throughout the fourteen Argentine
provinces were outraged that such a famous actor
should be accused of theft and murder; the countless
readers of evening papers knew that Gervasio Montenegro was a famous actor because he was accused of
theft and murder.

This priceless confusion was the exclusive doing of
that alert reporter Achilles Molinari, who, in solving
the mystery of Ibn Khaldun, had acquired so much
prestige. It was also thanks to Molinari that the police
allowed Gervasio Montenegro this highly unusual visit
to the jail where in cell 273 the sedentary detective
Isidro Parodi was serving time. (Molinari, with a gen-
erosity that fooled no one, attributed all his successes
to Parodi.)

A skeptic at heart, Montenegro had his doubts

about a detective who had formerly been a barber on Mexico Street, on the Southside of Buenos Aires, and was now a prison inmate. Montenegro's whole being, sensitive as a Stradivarius, shuddered at the prospect of this fateful visit. Still, he'd let himself be talked into it, well aware that he should avoid a falling out with Achilles Molinari, who, as Montenegro himself had put it, represented the fourth estate.

Parodi received the famous actor without looking up. In his slow, efficient way the detective was brewing maté in a small blue mug, which Montenegro was quite ready to sample. Parodi, however—no doubt owing to shyness—failed to offer him any. To put the detective at his ease, Montenegro patted him on the shoulder and lit a cigarette from a pack of Sublimes that lay on a stool.

"You've come early, don Montenegro. But I know what brings you. It's this business of the diamond."

"I see that these stout walls are no barrier to my fame," Montenegro hastened to remark.

"Correct. What better place than a jail cell to know what's going on all over the country—from the thieving in high places down to the cultural efforts of the lowliest radio actor."

"I share your aversion to the radio. As Margarita always said—Margarita Xirgu, you know—actors, those of us who have the stage in our blood, need the warmth of an audience. The microphone is cold, unnatural. Faced with that unsatisfactory gadget, I myself have experienced a loss of touch with my public."

"If I were you I'd forget about gadgets and being out of touch. I've read Molinari's articles. The boy's skillful with his pen, but all this fine writing and portrait sketching end up clear as mud. Why don't you tell me about it in your own way and leave out the art. Plain talk—that's what I like."

"Very well. As a matter of fact, that's exactly what I'm qualified for. Clarity is the prerogative of Latins. Nonetheless, you must allow me to cast a veil over a certain event which could compromise a society lady. The lady is from La Quiaca, in the far north, where, as you know, people of substance still live. *Laissez faire, laissez passer.* The stringent necessity of keeping untarnished the name of that lady who in the world's eyes is a darling of the finest drawing rooms—and for me an angel as well—forced me to interrupt my triumphant tour of the Indo-American republics. Out-and-out man of Buenos Aires that I am, I had looked forward—not without nostalgia—to the hour of my return, never for a moment believing it would be upset by circumstances which may well be termed criminal. In actual fact, the moment I arrived at Retiro Station, I was placed under arrest. I am now accused of theft and of a double murder. To crown the *accueil,* the men in blue stripped me of a jewel that I had acquired only hours before, in quite picturesque circumstances, while crossing the Rio Tercero. *Bref,* I detest pointless circumlocution. Let me tell my story *ab initio*—of course, without suppressing the lively irony that is now so much a part of modern life. I shall also allow myself a touch or two of the landscapist, a certain note of color.

"On the seventh of January, at four-fourteen A.M., soberly attired as a Bolivian Indian, I boarded the Pan-American Flyer in Mococo, cleverly shaking off— a question of savoir faire, my dear friend—my numerous but inept pursuers. The generous distribution of some autographed self-portraits succeeded in allaying, although not abolishing, the mistrust of the train's employees. I was given a compartment which I resigned myself to sharing with a stranger, who was obviously a Jew and who awoke on my arrival. I learned later that this intruder's name was Goliadkin and that he trafficked in diamonds. How on earth was I to know that this morose Israelite, whom the fates of the railway had bestowed on me, would plunge me into an unfathomable tragedy!

"The next day, while enjoying the heroic *capolavoro* of some Calchaquí chef, I was able to inspect with bonhomie the human fauna which populates that narrow world of the speeding train. My painstaking scrutiny began—*cherchez la femme*—with an interesting silhouette that even along fashionable Florida Street at eight P.M. would have merited a sidelong glance of male appreciation. On this topic I'm never mistaken. Later I found out that she was an exotic, exceptional woman; that she was the Baroness Puffendorf-Duvernois; that she was a woman of maturity with none of the deadly insipidity of, say, a schoolgirl; that she was a typical specimen of our time, having a trim body shaped by lawn tennis, a face perhaps a touch *basée* but subtly enhanced by creams and cosmetics—a woman, in a word, whose long spells of silence lent her elegance and whose slimness lent her height. She had, nonetheless, the *faible*—unforgivable in a true Duvernois—of flirting with Communism. At first, she succeeded in holding my interest, but soon I realized that her glittering veneer concealed a banal mind, and I requested poor Mr. Goliadkin to relieve me. She—and this is so typical of a woman—pretended not to have noticed the change. Still, I overheard a conversation between the *baronne* and another passenger, a certain Colonel Harrap, from Texas, in which she used the epithet 'nitwit' referring doubtless to *ce pauvre M. Goliadkin.* Let me return to Goliadkin. He was from Russia, a Jew, whose features in the photographic plate of my memory are decidedly weak. He was on the fair side, well built, and he had bulging eyes. He knew his place; he was forever rushing to open doors for me. On the other hand, it's impossible—albeit highly desirable—to forget the bearded, apoplectic Colonel Harrap, that typical product of a boisterous vulgar country which has reached gigantism but in which shades, nuances, are unknown. Shades, I might add, with which the lowliest urchin of any Neapolitan trattoria is familiar and which are the trademark of the Latin race."

"Never mind about Naples. If someone doesn't clear up this affair for you, you're going to find your-*self* sitting on one hell of a Vesuvius."

"I envy you your Benedictine reclusion, Mr. Parodi, but my life has been an errant one. I've sought light in the Balearics, color in Brindisi, and sophisticated sin in Paris. Also, like Renan, I've said a prayer on the Acropolis. I have squeezed life's juicy bunch of grapes the world over. But back to my story. In the Pullman car, while the unfortunate Goliadkin—after all, he was a Jew and so predestined to persecution—bore with resignation the *baronne's* tireless and tiring verbal wit, I, in the company of the young Catamarcan poet Bibiloni, enjoyed myself like an Athenian, expatiating upon poetry and the provinces. I confess now that the tanned—or, to be more exact, dusky—features of the young man who'd won the Vulcan Kerosene Stove Prize did not at first predispose me toward him. His pince-nez, his clip-on bow tie, his cream-colored gloves made me think that I had before me one of the many pedagogues bequeathed us by Sarmiento—that prophetic genius from whom it's absurd to demand the pedestrian virtue of foresight. However, the keen satisfaction with which he listened to a crown of triolets that I had dashed off a few days before demonstrated to me that he was one of the solid assets of our emerging literature. He was not one of those insufferable versifiers who take advantage of the first tête-à-tête to inflict on one the abortions of their pen. Bibiloni was thoughtful, discreet, and he did not squander the opportunity to keep quiet in the presence of his masters. I delighted him with the first of my odes to José Martí; just before my eleventh, however, I had to deprive him of the pleasure. The boredom that the incessant *baronne* inflicted on Goliadkin had rubbed off on my Catamarcan through an interesting phenomenon of psychological sympathy that I have often observed in other subjects. With my proverbial straightforwardness, which is the *apanage* of the man of the world, I hesitated not one instant before taking a radical course of action. I shook Bibiloni until he opened his eyes. Our conversation subsequently went into a decline. To give it new heights, I turned to the subject of fine tobaccos. That hit the mark. Bibiloni was all animation and interest. After rummaging in the inside pockets of his hunting jacket, he fished out a German cigar and, too shy to offer it to me, said that he had acquired it to smoke in his berth that night. I understood the innocent subterfuge. With a rapid movement I accepted the cigar and was quick to light it. Some pained memory crossed the young man's mind—at least, through my experience of reading faces, that's how I interpreted it. Sitting back comfortably in my armchair and exhaling blue mouthfuls of smoke, I asked him to speak of his triumphs. His interesting, swarthy face lit up. I listened to the old story of the writer, who struggles against the incomprehension of the middle classes and traverses the seas of life bearing his chimera on his shoulders. The Bibiloni family, after several decades of dedication to the pharmacopoeia of the sierra, managed to quit the borders of Catamarca and progress all the way to Bancalari. There, on the outskirts of Buenos Aires, the poet was born. His first teacher was nature—on the one hand, the bean patch of his paternal half-acre; on the other, the neighboring hen coops that the boy visited more than once on moonless nights, armed with a long rod for angling poultry. After a good grounding in primary studies at Kilometer 24, the poet returned to the soil. He understood the fruitful, virile labors of plow and harrow, which are worth more than any hollow applause, until the good judgment of Vulcan Stoves rescued him with an award for his book *Catamarqueñas (Memoirs of Provincial Life)*. The prize money permitted him to become acquainted with the province that he had sung with such affection. Now, enriched with ballads and villanelles, he was returning to his native Bancalari.

"We went into the dining car. Poor Goliadkin had to go and sit next to the *baronne;* across from them sat Father Brown and myself. The ecclesiastic's features were uninteresting. He had chestnut-colored hair and a round, vacant face. Nonetheless, I looked on him with certain envy. Those of us who've suffered the misfortune of losing the faith that the coal miner and the child still hold do not find in cold intelligence the comforting balm that the church holds out to its flock. Ultimately, what debt does our century, that white-haired blasé child, owe to the deep skepticism of Anatole France and Júlio Dantas? All of us, my esteemed Parodi, could do with a bit of innocence and simplicity.

"I remember the conversation of that evening with some confusion. The *baronne,* using as a pretext the midsummer heat, kept lowering her neckline and pressing herself against Goliadkin—just to excite me. The Jew, little accustomed to this sort of advance, vainly shrank from the contact and, conscious of the poor figure he was cutting, spoke nervously on subjects that couldn't have been of interest to anyone—such as the downward trend of the diamond market, the impossibility of substituting a fake diamond for a real one, and something about the business of running a boutique. Father Brown, who seemed oblivious of the difference between the dining car of a deluxe express train and a congregation of defenseless parishioners, repeated I forget which paradox on the need to lose the soul in order to save it. It was the mindless Byzantinism of theologians, who have obscured the clarity of the Gospels.

"Noblesse oblige. To have ignored the *baronne's* lascivious invitations would have meant making a fool of myself. That same night I glided on tiptoe to her compartment and, squatting down on my haunches, my dream-filled head pressed to the door, eye to the keyhole, I hummed confidentially, 'Mon ami Pierrot.' Out of this peaceful lull that comes to every soldier in the throes of life's struggle, I was startled by the old-fashioned puritanism of Colonel Harrap. In fact, this bearded old man, this relic of the piratical Spanish-American War, took me by the shoulders, raised me a considerable height, and dumped me unceremoniously in front of the gentlemen's toilet. My response was quick. I got in and shut the door in his face. There I remained for close on two hours, lending a sharp ear to his confused threats, uttered in faulty Spanish. When I abandoned my refuge, the way was clear. 'I'm free!' I exclaimed to myself, and instantly retired to my compartment. Obviously, lady luck was with me. In the compartment was the *baronne,* waiting for me. She literally leaped on seeing me. In the background, Goliadkin was putting on his jacket. The *baronne,* with quick feminine intuition, realized that Goliadkin's presence destroyed the intimate mood that is so necessary to lovers. She left without a word to him. I know my temperament. I knew that if I ran into the colonel again, we'd fight a duel. This would be most awkward on a train. Besides, however difficult it is to accept, the fact is the age of dueling is no more. I opted for my bed.

"How strange the servility of the Hebrew! My entrance had frustrated who knows what unprovoked intention of Goliadkin; nevertheless, from that moment on, he became exceedingly cordial to me, forced me to accept his Italian cigars, and began lavishing attention on me.

"The next day, everybody was in a bad humor. For my part, ever sensitive to psychological moods, I tried to lift the spirits of my table companions by telling some of Roberto Payró's anecdotes and one or two of Marcos Sastre's perfect epigrams. Madame Puffendorf-Duvernois, indignant over the episode of the night before, was plainly irritable. Apparently, some echo of her *mésaventure* had reached Father Brown's ears. He treated her with a curtness that was altogether unworthy of the ecclesiastical tonsure.

"After lunch, I taught Colonel Harrap a lesson. To show him that his faux pas had had no effect on our cordial relations, I offered him one of Goliadkin's stogies, and I gave myself the pleasure of lighting it for him. A slap in the face with a white glove!

"That night, the third of our journey, young

Bibiloni disappointed me. I'd been looking forward to telling him about a few of my adventures in gallantry —the ones I don't often share with the first man I meet. But he was not in his compartment. It upset me to think that a Catamarcan half-breed could have slipped into Baroness Puffendorf's compartment. Sometimes I can be like Sherlock Holmes. Cleverly eluding the conductor, whom I bribed with an interesting example of Paraguayan numismatics, I tried— cold-blooded hound of the Baskervilles—to listen in to, nay, to spy on, what was taking place in that compartment. (The colonel had retired early.) Complete silence and darkness were the harvest of my inspection. But my anxiety was not to last. To my surprise I saw the *baronne* leaving Father Brown's compartment. For a moment I was overcome by violent feelings of rebellion, forgivable in a man whose veins pulse with the fiery blood of Montenegros. And then it came to me. The *baronne* had been making her confession. Her hair was in disarray, her attire was ascetic—a flaming-red nightgown, silver ballerina slippers with gold pompoms. She wore no makeup and, woman to the core, she fled to her compartment so that I should not come upon her without her cosmetic mask. I lit up one of young Bibiloni's bad cigars and beat a philosophical retreat.

"Surprisingly, in spite of the lateness of the hour, Goliadkin was still up. I smiled. Two days of railroad-car conviviality had been enough for the dull Jew to begin imitating the noctambulism of the man about town. Goliadkin's new habit, of course, did not suit him at all. He was beside himself, nervous. Heedless of my nodding off and my yawns, he inflicted on me all the details of his insignificant and probably apocryphal life story. He claimed to have been stable master and then lover of Princess Clavdia Fiodorovna. With a cynicism that reminded me of the most daring pages of Gil Blas de Santillana, he claimed that, taking advantage of the trust of the princess and of her confessor, Father Abramowicz, he had stolen a great, old, rough diamond, a nonpareil that but for the minor defect of being uncut would have been the most valuable in the world. Twenty years yawned between him and that night of passion, robbery, and flight. In the interim, the Red tide had expelled the despoiled lady and her untrustworthy stable master from the empire of the czars. On those very borders the threefold odyssey began—the princess in search of her daily bread; Goliadkin in search of the princess to restore the diamond to her; and a gang of international thieves in search of the stolen diamond and Goliadkin. Goliadkin, in the mines of South Africa, in Brazilian laboratories, in the bazaars of Bolivia, had known danger and poverty. But he never tried to sell the diamond, which was his scourge and his hope. In time, Princess Clavdia became for Goliadkin a symbol of that Russia, once beneficent and grand, which had been crushed by bureaucrats and utopians. Not finding the princess made him love her more and more. Then, not long ago, he discovered she was in the Argentine, running —without giving up her aristocratic *morgue*—a prosperous establishment in Avellaneda. Only at the last moment did Goliadkin remove the diamond from its secret hiding place. Now that he knew where the princess was, he would rather have died than have lost it.

"Naturally, such a long story from a man who, by his own confession, had been a stable groom and a thief, made me uneasy. With my typical frankness, I allowed myself to express a discreet doubt about the existence of the jewel. My thrust went home. Goliadkin took two identical boxes out of an imitation alligator valise and opened one of them. There could be no doubt. There in its velvet nest glittered a true brother of the Koh-i-noor. Nothing human is strange to me. I sympathized with poor Goliadkin, who had once shared the fleeting bed of a Fiodorovna and who now, in a creaking railway car, confided his troubles to an Argentine gentleman who would certainly offer his services to help him reach the princess. I warmed him to the idea, telling him that pursuit by a band of thieves was less serious than pursuit by the police. At once fraternal and magnanimous, I mentioned that a raid on the Salón Doré had caused my name—one of the country's oldest—to be entered in heaven knows what infamous police blotter.

"How odd was my friend's psychology! Twenty years without seeing his beloved's face and now, almost on the eve of happiness, his mind was besieged by doubts.

"In spite of a reputation as a bohemian—justified *d'ailleurs*—I'm a man of regular habits. It was late, and I was no longer able to sleep. In my mind I kept turning over the story of the diamond so near and the princess so far away. Goliadkin, obviously moved by the noble frankness of my words, couldn't sleep either. At any rate, he tossed and turned in his upper berth all night.

"Morning had two surprises in store for me. First, a distant view of the pampa, which spoke to my soul as an Argentine and an artist. A ray of sun lit up the countryside. Beneath the lavish blessing of life-giving sunshine, the fence posts, the wires, the thistles wept with joy. The sky grew suddenly immense, and the plain glowed in the light. The heifers seemed to be dressed in new clothes.

"My second surprise was of a psychological nature. Over our cordial breakfast mugs, Father Brown showed us clearly that the cross need not be at odds with the sword. With all the authority and prestige of his tonsure, he berated Colonel Harrap, whom he called (and quite rightly in my opinion) an ass and a beast. He also told him that he was only good for bullying poor nobodies, and that in the presence of a real man he was careful to maintain his distance. Harrap uttered not a peep.

"Only later did I understand the full meaning of the priest's reprimand. I found out that Bibiloni had disappeared that night. The man of the pen had been that military lunatic's poor nobody."

"Let me get a word in edgewise, friend Montenegro," said Parodi. "That strange train of yours—didn't it stop anywhere?"

"Where do you come from, my dear friend Parodi? Don't you know that the Pan-American runs nonstop from Bolivia to Buenos Aires? Let me continue. That evening the conversation was boring. No one wanted to speak of anything other than Bibiloni's disappearance. Indeed, some passenger or other remarked that the much-touted safety that Anglo-Saxon capitalists claim for railway trains was open to doubt after this turn of events. Without disagreeing, I pointed out that Bibiloni's action might well have been the result of absentmindedness, which is so typical of the poetic temperament, and that I myself, in the thrall of a chimera, was often in the clouds. These hypotheses, which seemed plausible by the sober light of day, began to fade with the last pirouette of the sun. When night fell, everything was tinged with melancholy. From time to time from out of the blackness came the insistent complaints of an unseen owl, mocking the dry cough of a sick man. It was the moment perhaps when in his mind each passenger turned over distant memories or experienced some vague dark fear of the nether life. In unison, all the wheels of the train seemed to drum out *Bi-bi-lo-ni-has-been-killed, Bi-bi-lo-ni-has-been-killed, Bi-bi-lo-ni-has-been-killed.*

"That night, after dinner, Goliadkin—doubtless to relieve the anguished mood that had taken possession of the dining car—made the mistake of challenging me to a two-handed game of poker. His need to measure himself against me was such that he turned down with surprising stubbornness the suggestion of the *baronne* and the colonel to play a foursome. Naturally, Goliadkin's hopes were dashed. The haunter of the Salón Doré did not disappoint his public. At first, the cards did not favor me, but later, in spite of my fatherly warnings, Goliadkin lost all his money—three hundred and fifty pesos, forty cents—which the cops, quite arbitrarily, later lifted from me. I shall never forget that duel. The plebeian versus the man of the world, greed versus detachment, the Jew versus the Aryan. What a valuable picture for my mental gallery! Goliadkin, looking for a last chance to break even, suddenly left the dining car. He was not long in returning with his imitation crocodile valise. He drew out one of the two boxes and put it on the table. He suggested playing for the three hundred pesos against the diamond. I did not deny him this last chance. I dealt the cards. I held a full house; we showed our hands. Princess Fiodorovna's diamond was mine. The Jew withdrew, *navré.* What a moment!

"*A tout seigneur, tout honneur.* The gloved-hand applause of the Baroness Puffendorf, who had followed her champion's victory with ill-concealed interest, crowned the spectacle. As the saying goes in the Salón

50

Doré, Montenegro does not do things by halves. I had made up my mind. I called for the waiter and ipso facto asked for the wine list. A quick look at it counseled that the occasion called for Champagne Applefizz—a half bottle. I drank a toast with the *baronne*.

"You can always tell a playboy. After such an adventure, no one else would have slept a wink. But suddenly, insensitive to the spell of the tête-à-tête, I craved the solitude of my compartment. I yawned an excuse and withdrew. My fatigue was overwhelming. I remember making my way, half asleep, along the train's endless passageways. Disregarding the regulations invented by Anglo-Saxon companies to restrict the freedom of the passenger, I finally entered the first free compartment and, faithful guardian of my jewel, bolted the door.

"I confess without a blush, my dear Parodi, that night I slept with my clothes on. I fell like a log into the berth.

"All mental effort brings about its own retribution. The whole night I was subjected to a disturbing nightmare. The *ritornello* of that nightmare had Goliadkin's mocking voice, and it kept repeating, 'I won't tell you where the diamond is.' I awoke with a start. My first movement was to check an inner pocket. The case was there. In it was the genuine nonpareil. Relieved, I opened the window. Light. Fresh air. The mad dawn chattering of birds. A misty January dawn—a sleepy dawn, still wrapped in sheets of whitish haze.

"From this morning poetry, I was suddenly yanked into the prose of life by a knock at my door. I opened. It was Assistant Chief Grondona. He asked what I was doing in that compartment and, without waiting for my answer, he told me to go back to my own. I've always been like a swallow for finding my way. Unbelievable as it may seem, my compartment was next door. I found it a shambles. Grondona suggested that I stop feigning astonishment. Later, I learned what you must have read in the newspapers. Goliadkin had been thrown from the train. A conductor heard his cry and sounded the alarm. In San Martín, the police came aboard. Everybody accused me, even the *baronne*—no doubt out of spite. And here's a detail that reveals what an acute observer I am. In the thick of the police bustle, I noticed that the colonel had shaved off his beard."

II

A week later, Montenegro appeared at the prison again. In the quiet comfort of the back of the police van he'd boned up on no less than fourteen country-bumpkin jokes and seven of García Lorca's acrostics—all for the edification of his new protégé, the inhabitant of cell 273, Isidro Parodi. But once the two were together the stubborn barber took a grimy playing card out of his regulation cap, and he proposed—or rather, imposed—a two-handed game of *truco.*

"All games are my game," said Montenegro. "At my forebears' estate, in its battlemented castle whose towers are reflected in the flowing Paraná, I have accepted the gaucho's embracing fellowship and shared his rustic pastime. Indeed, my motto 'It's all in the cards' was the fear of every *truco* player the length and breadth of the Paraná delta."

Very soon, Montenegro—who lost badly in the two hands they played—was forced to admit that *truco,* owing to its very simplicity, could never hold the attention of a devotee of chemin de fer and auction bridge.

Ignoring him, Parodi said, "Look, in return for this lesson in *truco* that you have taught an aging man who's no longer much good, even against a nobody, I'm going to tell you a story. It's about a very brave, though star-crossed man—a man for whom I have enormous respect."

"I grasp your drift, dear Parodi," said Montenegro, helping himself unselfconsciously to a Sublime. "This respect does you great credit."

"I wasn't thinking of you. No, I speak of a deceased man whom I never knew, a foreigner from Russia, the coachman or groom of a lady who owned a valuable diamond. That lady was a princess in her own country, but love obeys no rules. The young man, dizzy from so much luck, had one weakness—it can happen to anyone—and he made off with the diamond. When he realized what he had done it was too late. The Maximalist revolution had cast the two of them into different corners of the world. A band of thieves, first in a small town in South Africa, then in another in Brazil, sought to snatch the jewel from him. They couldn't. The man managed to hide it. He didn't want it for himself; he wanted to return it to the lady. After years of vicissitude, he learned that the lady was in Buenos Aires. It was dangerous to travel with a diamond, but the man did not flinch. The thieves pursued him onto the train, one disguised as a monk, another as a soldier, another as a man from the provinces, and another had her face touched up. Among the passengers was a countryman of ours, a simpleton, an actor. This man, as he had spent his life among disguises, saw nothing strange in these people. Still, the farce was obvious. The group was too random. A priest who takes his name from fiction, a Catamarcan from Bancalari, a woman who pretends to be a baroness because there's a princess in the affair, an old man who from one day to the next loses his beard and who is able to lift you 'to a considerable height,' despite your hundred and eighty pounds, and lock you up in a toilet. They were a determined bunch. They had four nights in which to do the trick. On the first night, you turned up in Goliadkin's compartment and blew it for them. The second night, you saved him again, unwittingly; the woman had wormed her way into his room on the pretext of love, but on your arrival she was forced to beat a retreat. The third night, while you were glued to the baroness's door, the Catamarcan held Goliadkin up. Bibiloni botched it. Goliadkin threw him off the train. That was why the Jew acted nervously and twisted and turned in his bed. He was thinking about what had happened and what was to come; he was probably thinking about the fourth night —the last and the most dangerous of all. He recalled the priest's words about those who lose their souls to save them. He decided to let himself be killed and so lose the diamond to save it. You had mentioned your police record; he realized that if he were killed you'd be the prime suspect. On that fourth night he showed off two cases so that the thieves would think he had two diamonds, a real and a fake one. In the presence of everyone he lost the fake to someone who's hopeless at cards. The thieves figured that he wanted them to believe he had gambled away the real jewel. Slipping a mickey into your cider, they put you to sleep. Then they got into the Jew's compartment and ordered him to hand over the diamond. In your dreams you heard him repeating that he didn't know where it was. To confuse them, he may also have told them that

54

you had it. The trick worked. Early that morning the devils killed that brave man, but the diamond was safe with you. And so, as soon as the train arrived in Buenos Aires, the police nabbed you and saw to it that the jewel was handed over to its rightful owner.

"Maybe Goliadkin thought his life wasn't worth living out. Twenty cruel years had befallen the princess, who now ran a house of ill fame. In his place, I too would have had my misgivings."

Montenegro lit a second Sublime. "It's the old, old story," he remarked. "Straggling intellect once again confirms the artist's intuition. All along, I had my doubts about Madame Puffendorf-Duvernois, Bibiloni, Father Brown, and—most especially—Colonel Harrap. Don't worry, my dear Parodi, I shan't be long in revealing my solution to the authorities."

Quequén, Province of Buenos Aires,
February 5, 1942

The God
of the Bulls

To the memory of the poet Alexander Pope

I

With the manly frankness so characteristic of him, the poet José Formento told the ladies and gentlemen gathered at the Casa de Arte (at the corner of Florida and Tucumán): "Nothing gladdens my heart more than the verbal contests between my master Carlos Anglada and our eighteenth-centuryish Gervasio Montenegro. Marinetti versus Lord Byron. The Buick versus the aristocratic tilbury. The machine gun versus the sword." These contests gave pleasure to the principals as well, who, moreover, were exceedingly fond of each other. As soon as he learned about the disappearance of the letters, Montenegro (since marrying the Princess Fiodorovna, he had retired from the theater and was devoting his leisure both to the writing of a bulky historical novel and to the pursuit of criminal investigations) offered Carlos Anglada the full range of his perspicacity and prestige, but he pointed out the advisability of a visit to cell 273, where for the moment his collaborator Isidro Parodi was confined.

Unlike the reader, Parodi was unacquainted with

Carlos Anglada. Don Isidro had not looked into the sonnets of *The Senile Pagodas* (1912) or the pantheistic odes of *I Am All Others* (1921) or the capital letters of *I Spy with My Little Eye* (1928) or the telluric novel *The Cahiers of a Cowhand* (1931) or a single one of the *Hymns for Millionaires* (five hundred numbered copies, plus the popular Catholic Boy Scouts Press edition, 1934) or the *Antiphon of the Loaves and Fishes* (1935) or —outrageous as it may seem—the learned imprint of Test Tube Editions, Inc. (*Loose Leaves of a Diver, Collected and Edited by the Minotaur*, 1939).* It pains us to confess that in the course of twenty years of imprisonment, Parodi had not had time to study *Carlos Anglada's Itinerary, The Genesis and Development of a Lyric Poet.* In this indispensable study, José Formento, advised by the master himself, documents Anglada's various periods: his modernist beginnings; his assimilation (at times transcription) of Joaquín Belda; his pantheistic fervor of 1921 when, thirsting for complete communion with nature, the poet rejected any sort of footwear and limped, bruised and bleeding, among the flower beds of his attractive villa out in Vicente López; his rejection of impersonal intellectualism—those now celebrated years when Anglada, in the company of a governess and a Chilean version of D. H. Lawrence, paid many an intrepid visit to the lakes in Palermo Park, childishly dressed in a sailor suit and armed with a hoop and a scooter; his Nietzschean reawakening, which germinated in *Hymns for Mil-*

*Carlos Anglada's commendable bibliography also comprises the following: the crude naturalistic novel *Drawing-Room Flesh* (1914), the magnanimous palinode *Drawing-Room Spirit* (1914), the long since superseded manifesto *Words to Pegasus* (1917), the travel notes *In the Beginning Was the Pullman Car* (1923), and the four numbered numbers of the review *Zero* (1924–27).

lionaires, a work that was based on an article by Azorín and upheld aristocratic values but which Anglada would ultimately disown when he became the popular catechumen of the Eucharistic Congress; and finally, his altruistic forays into the provinces, where the master submits to the scalpel of criticism the latest unpublished generation of poets, for whom Test Tube Editions, Inc., provides a forum thanks to its nearly one hundred subscribers and projected handful of thinnish booklets.

Carlos Anglada in person was not as formidable as his bibliography or his photograph. Don Isidro, who was brewing himself a maté in his blue mug, looked up and saw the man—tall, sturdy, red-faced, prematurely bald, his stubborn eyes frowning, his bristling mustache dyed. He wore, as José Formento used to remark jovially, a checked suit. He was followed by a man who, up close, looked like Anglada himself seen from a distance—the baldness, the eyes, the mustache, the burliness, the checked suit were the same but on a smaller scale. The alert reader will have guessed by now that this young man was José Formento, Anglada's apostle and gospel-spreader. Formento's task was by no means dull. Anglada's versatility would have defeated a less self-denying and tireless disciple than the author of *Pissabed* (1929), *Notes of a Poultry Wholesaler* (1932), *Odes for Managers* (1934), and *Sunday in the Sky* (1936). As everyone knew, Formento worshiped his master, who reciprocated with a cordial condescension that included the occasional friendly scolding. Formento was not only Anglada's disciple but also his secretary—that *bonne à tout faire* whom great writers retain to punctuate their masterpieces and to clean up the odd orthographical error.

Anglada went straight to the point. "Please excuse

me," he said. "I speak with the frankness of a motorcycle. I've come at the suggestion of Gervasio Montenegro. I want to make that perfectly clear. I don't believe —and I never will—that a convicted felon's the proper person to solve criminal cases. My problem is straightforward. I live, as everyone knows, out in Vicente López. In my study—in my metaphor workshop, to be more precise—there's a safe. This locked polyhedron holds—or, rather, used to hold—a packet of letters. That is no mystery. My correspondent and admirer is Mariana Ruiz Villalba de Muñagorri—Moncha to her intimates. My cards are on the table. Despite slanderous rumor, there has been no carnal commerce between us. We move on a higher plane—emotional and intellectual. I'm afraid no Argentine would ever understand a relationship like this. Mariana is a beautiful spirit. And what is more, she's a beautiful woman. This superbly endowed creature has an antenna sensitive to every modern vibration. My firstborn work, *The Senile Pagodas,* inspired her to compose sonnets. I corrected her pentameters. The presence of a few alexandrines among them showed a true vocation for free verse. In fact, she now cultivates the prose essay. She has written 'A Rainy Day,' 'My Dog Bob,' 'The First Day of Spring,' 'The Battle of Chacabuco,' 'Why I Like Picasso,' 'Why I Like My Garden,' and so forth and so on. To be brief, let me descend like a diver to the fine points of detection, which is more in your line. As everyone knows, I'm essentially gregarious. On the fourteenth of August, I opened the maw of my villa to an interesting group of people: all Test Tube writers and subscribers. The former demanded the publication of their manuscripts; the latter, a refund of their money. In circumstances like these, I'm as happy as a submarine in water. The lively party went on until two in the morning. If nothing else, I'm a warrior. Throwing up a barricade of armchairs and stools, I managed to save a good part of the crockery. Formento, more like Ulysses than Diomedes, tried to placate the polemicists by bringing in a trayful of cold cuts and orangeade. Poor Formento! All he succeeded in doing was to provide my detractors with more ammunition. When the last *pompier* had left, Formento, with a devotion I shall never forget, poured a bucket of water over my head, thus restoring my wit to its customary three-thousand watts. During my collapse, I devised an acrobatic poem called 'Standing Up on an Impulse.' The last line ran, 'I shot at Death from point-blank range.' It would have been fatal to have lost that nugget of my subconscious mind. Without a mention of the morrow, I dismissed my disciple. Formento, in the thick of the verbal battle, had lost his change purse. To be quite frank, he required my assistance for his return journey to Saavedra. The key to my inviolable Diebold lies in the stronghold of my pocket. I extracted the key, thrust it home, and gave it a turn. I found the solicited funds but not my letters from Moncha— sorry, from Mariana Ruiz Villalba de Muñagorri. The blow did not fell me. Eternally vigilant in the ancient citadel of Thought, I searched the house and grounds from the water heater down to the cesspool. The results of my efforts were negative."

"I confirm that the letters aren't at the villa," said the thick voice of Formento. "On the morning of the fifteenth, I returned with a fact from the *Shorter Illustrated Larousse* that my master required for his research. I volunteered to look through the house again. I turned up nothing. No, that's not quite true. I found something of value for Mr. Anglada and for the nation.

It was treasure that the poet, in his absentmindedness, had mislaid in the basement—four hundred and ninety-seven copies of the out-of-print *Cahiers of a Cowhand.*"

"You must excuse my disciple's literary enthusiasm," Carlos Anglada quickly put in. "This scholarly discovery can't possibly be of interest to a mind like yours, narrowly confined as it is to police matters. The fact is this: the letters have disappeared. In the hands of an unscrupulous person these outpourings from a great lady, these records of both gray and sentimental matter could precipitate an enormous scandal. We're dealing here with a human document that combines style—modeled after my own—with the delicate intimacy of a woman of the world. *Bref,* wonderful bait for piratical Chilean publishing houses."

II

One week later, an enormous Cadillac stopped on Las Heras Street before the state penitentiary. The small door in the main gate opened. A gentleman wearing a gray jacket, fancy trousers, light-colored gloves, and carrying a walking stick with a handle in the shape of a dog's head got out of the car. With resolute step, slightly old-fashioned in his elegance, he entered the prison grounds.

Assistant Chief Grondona received him with fawning subservience. The gentleman accepted a Brazilian cigar and allowed himself to be led to cell 273. Don Isidro, as soon as he saw him, concealed a pack of Sublimes under his regulation cap and in a gentle voice said, "My, isn't flesh selling well in Avellaneda! It's a trade that keeps many a good man in trim, but on you it's fattening."

"Touché, my dear Parodi, touché. I confess I'm a trifle overweight," said Montenegro between two blue mouthfuls of smoke. "The princess begs me to kiss your hand. Also, our mutual friend Carlos Anglada— a wit, if ever there was one, although he lacks the discipline of the true Latin—remembers you. *Inter nos,* he remembers you all too often. Only yesterday he stormed into my office. By his wheezing and the way he slammed the door, I—a reader of physiognomies— deduced in a twinkling that Carlos Anglada was on edge. I understood why at once. Traffic congestion destroys serenity of mind. Of course, you, a wiser man, have chosen well—solitude, routine, absence of stimuli. Here in the heart of the city your little oasis is another world. Our friend hasn't your character. The merest chimera terrifies him. Frankly, I thought he was made of sterner stuff. At first, he took the loss of the letters with the stoicism of a playboy. But yesterday I discovered that this was little more than a façade. The man has been wounded, *blessé.* In my office, over a bottle of 1934 Maraschino, veiled in the bracing smoke of cigars, he stripped himself of all disguise. I understand his fears. Publication of Moncha's correspondence would be a rude blow to society. The woman's *hors concours,* my dear friend. Physical beauty, breeding, fortune, position—she's a modern spirit in a Murano vase. Pitifully, Carlos Anglada insists that the publication of these letters would bring about his ruin and the distinctly unhealthy *besogne* of finishing off the irascible Muñagorri in a duel. In spite of this, my esteemed Parodi, I beg you, keep a level head. My genius for organization has come to grips with the problem. As a first step I've invited Carlos Anglada and Formento to spend a few days at La Moncha, Muñagorri's breeding ranch. Noblesse oblige—we must admit that Muñagorri's work has brought progress to a whole sector of El Pilar. You really should come out and see the place. It's one of the few estates where the tradition of native culture is kept alive and thriving. In spite of the intrusion of the owner of the house, an absolute tyrant with thoroughly old-fashioned views, no cloud will darken this friendly gathering. Mariana will do the honors—with her customary grace, of course. I can assure you that this journey is no mere artistic caprice of mine. Our personal physician, Dr. Mugica, prescribes a radical treatment for my *surmenage*. Despite Mariana's cordial insistence, the princess will not be able to join us. Her various activities in Avellaneda keep her busy. For my part, however, I intend to extend my *villégiature* until the beginning of spring. As you've just seen, I haven't shrunk from swallowing the bitter pill. I leave in your hands the details of the detective work—the recovery of the letters. Tomorrow at ten, our happy motorcade proceeds from the Rivadavia cenotaph, en route to La Moncha, intoxicated with limitless horizons, with freedom."

With a precise movement, Gervasio Montenegro consulted his gold Vacheron et Constantin. "Time is money," he exclaimed. "I've promised to pay visits to Colonel Harrap and Reverend Brown, your confrères in this penal institution. A short time ago, at the women's prison on San Juan Street, I visited the Baroness Puffendorf-Duvernois, *née* Pratolongo. Her dignity has not suffered, but her Abyssinian tobacco is abominable."

On the fifth of September, in the late afternoon, a visitor with a black armband and umbrella entered cell 273. He spoke without hesitation, but beneath his funereal liveliness don Isidro sensed that the man was worried.

"Here I stand, crucified like the sun at the hour it sets." José Formento pointed vaguely in the direction of an airshaft that led to the laundry room. "You may brand me a Judas, busy with social calls while my master endures persecution. But my motive for coming here concerns something entirely different. I have come to demand of you—or, better still, to beg you— to use every last bit of the influence you've acquired during so many years of living close to the law. Without love, charity is unviable. It's as Carlos Anglada said in his appeal to the Agrarian Youth Movement: to understand the tractor, one must love the tractor. To understand Carlos Anglada, it's necessary to love Carlos Anglada. Surely the master's books will prove useless in any criminal investigation. Here's a copy of my *Carlos Anglada's Itinerary.* In it, the man who hoodwinks the critics yet interests the police is revealed as impulsive, almost as a child."

Formento opened the book at random and thrust it into Parodi's hands. Parodi, true enough, saw a photograph of Carlos Anglada, bald and brimming with energy, dressed as a sailor.

"As a photographer," said Parodi, "you may be unrivaled— I don't question that. But what I need to be told is what happened since the night of August twenty-ninth. I'd also like to know how all those people got on. I've read Molinari's pieces; he has a good head on his shoulders, that boy, but one gets bogged down in so much photographic detail. Don't be upset, young man; just tell me everything, step by step."

"I'll give you a snapshot of the facts. We arrived at the ranch on the twenty-fourth. Plenty of cordiality and harmony. Señora Mariana—in a Redfern riding outfit, Patou cape, Hermès boots, Elizabeth Arden 'Outdoor Girl' makeup—received us with her usual simple grace. Until well after nightfall, the Anglada-Montenegro duo argued about the sunset. Anglada claimed it was inferior to the headlights of an automobile devouring the macadam. Montenegro said it was inferior to a Petrarchan sonnet. In the end, both factions drowned their polemical spirits in vermouth with bitters. Señor Manuel Muñagorri, appeased by Montenegro's tact, appeared to be resigned to our visit. At eight o'clock sharp, the governess—a truly coarse blonde, believe me—brought in Pampa, the happy couple's only child. From the top of the stairs, Señora Mariana held out her arms to the boy, and he, dressed as a gaucho with a dagger and breeches, ran to bury himself in her maternal caress. It was an unforgettable scene, even if repeated nightly, and it demonstrates the permanence of family ties despite an atmosphere of bohemian worldliness. At once, the governess took Pampa away. Muñagorri explained that the whole science of bringing up children was contained in the Solomonic rule, 'Spare the rod and spoil the child.' I'm positive that in order to make the boy wear the *chiripá* and dagger, the father had to keep putting that rule into practice.

"On the afternoon of the twenty-ninth, from a position on the terrace, we watched a solemn, splendid parade of bulls. We were indebted to Señora Mariana for this rural tableau. Had it not been for her, this, and other pleasant experiences, would never have been. With a man's candor, I must confess that Señor Muñagorri—for all his apparent experience as a breeder—was a retiring, unsociable host. He barely addressed a word to us. He preferred speaking to foremen and cowhands, and he showed more interest in the forthcoming Palermo Cattle Show than in the marvelous conjunction of nature and art, the pampa and Carlos Anglada, that was taking place on his own property minute after minute. While the animals filed by below, dark in the death of the sun, above on the terrace the group of men and women became more voluble and verbose. A single exclamation from Montenegro about the majesty of bulls was enough to spur Anglada's wit. The master, quoting himself, improvised one of those spontaneous lyrical outbursts that never fails to astound both historian and grammarian, both the cold rationalist and the warm heart. He said that in earlier ages, bulls were sacred animals; before that, priests and kings; still earlier, gods. He said that the same sun that shone on this parade of bulls had witnessed, in Cretan labyrinths, the parades of men who had been sentenced to death for having blasphemed against the bull. He spoke of men for whom immersion in a bull's warm blood bestowed immortality. Montenegro tried to evoke a bloody spectacle of bulls with balls stuck on their horns that he had witnessed in the arenas of Nîmes under the dying Provençal sun. But Muñagorri, the sworn enemy of all expansiveness and flair, said that on the subject of bulls Anglada was little more than a shopkeeper. Enthroned on an enormous wicker armchair, the cattleman stated the obvious—that he had been brought up among bulls, and that they were peaceful and even cowardly animals, though extremely powerful. So as to convince Anglada, Muñagorri was apparently trying to hypnotize him. He didn't take his eyes off Anglada for a moment. And that's where we left the master and Muñagorri—in full polemical bliss. Guided by our incomparable hostess, Señora Mariana, Montenegro and I were able to appreciate each and every detail of the ranch's electric generator. The gong sounded, we sat down to dinner, and we finished the beef course before the polemicists joined us. It was obvious that the master had been the victor; Muñagorri, sullen and vanquished, didn't speak a single word during the whole of dinner.

"The following day he invited me to see the village of El Pilar. There were just the two of us, and we went in his two-wheeled buggy. As a true Argentine, I delighted in our escapade across typical dusty pampa. The paternal sun lavished its kindly rays on our heads. The postal service reaches even these backcountry dirt roads. And while Muñagorri was sponging up inflammable liquids in the local saloon, I entrusted to a mail slot a filial greeting to my publisher, written on the back of a picture of me dressed as a gaucho.

"The return journey was unpleasant. The drunkard's clumsiness increased the perils of our *via crucis*. But I confess upon my honor that I took pity on that slave of alcohol, and I forgave him the ugly spectacle he was making of himself. He punished the horse as if it were his son. The buggy was in grave danger of rolling over, and more than once I feared for my life.

"Back at the estate, some flaxseed compresses and the reading of an old manifesto of Marinetti's restored my equilibrium. Now, don Isidro, we arrive at the evening of the crime. It was foreshadowed by an unpleasant incident. Muñagorri, ever faithful to the teachings of Solomon, rained a hail of blows on the seat of

Pampa's pants—all because the boy, misled by the false claims of exotic fashion, refused to wear the native whip and dagger. Miss Bilham, the governess, not knowing her place, prolonged the unpleasant episode by launching into a bitter recrimination of Muñagorri. I have no hesitation in stating that the nanny intervened in this uncontrolled manner because she was out for another position. Montenegro, who's an absolute fox for sniffing out beautiful souls, had offered her some kind of job in Avellaneda. We all withdrew in a state of nerves. The hostess, the master, and I went for a walk out as far as the water tank. Montenegro retired within the house in the company of the governess. Muñagorri, obsessed by the coming cattle show, went to watch another promenade of bulls. Solitude and work are the twin staffs upon which the true man of letters leans; I took advantage of a bend in the path to take leave of my friends, and I made my way to my bedroom, a truly wonderful windowless refuge where not even the least echo of the outside world penetrates. Putting on the light, I harnessed myself to the furrow of my popular translation of *La soirée avec M. Teste.* But it proved impossible to work. Montenegro and Miss Bilham were chatting away in the next room. I hadn't shut my door out of fear of offending Miss Bilham as well as of suffocating. The other door of my room opens, as you know, out into the kitchen's steamy backyard.

"I heard a cry. It hadn't come from Miss Bilham's room. I thought I recognized the incomparable voice of Señora Mariana. Down corridors and stairways I raced to reach the terrace. There, against the sunset —solemn, like the great natural actress she is—Señora Mariana pointed to the terrible scene which, to my eternal regret, I shall always remember. Down below, like the previous day, the bulls had paraded past; up on the terrace, like the previous day, the ranch's owner had presided over the slow promenade. But this time the bulls were on show for one man alone, and that man was dead. A knife had pierced the woven pattern of the back of the chair. Held in place by the chair's arms, the corpse sat upright. Horror-struck, Anglada confirmed that the unbelievable murder had been committed with the child's miniature dagger."

"Tell me, don Formento, how do you think the killer got hold of the weapon?"

"It's a mystery. After having attacked his father, the boy threw a tantrum, then chucked his gaucho gear behind the hortensias."

"I should have guessed. But how do you explain the presence of the toy whip in Anglada's room?"

"Easily, but with explanations no police detective would understand. As the photograph which you have seen shows, in Anglada's protean life there was a stage one could term infantile. Even today, as a champion of international copyright and art for art's sake, he feels the irresistible attraction that toys have for an adult."

IV

On the ninth of September, two women in mourning entered cell 273. One was a blonde, with powerful hips and full lips; the other, who dressed more discreetly, was small, thin, and flat-chested, and she had short, slender legs.

"From what I've heard, you must be Muñagorri's widow," said don Isidro, addressing the blonde.

"What a gaff!" the other woman said in a shrill voice. "He's already off on the wrong foot. How can she be me when she's only keeping me company? She's the nanny, Miss Bilham. I'm Mrs. Muñagorri."

Parodi offered them his two stools and sat on the cot.

Mariana went on in no particular hurry. "What an absolutely divine little room—not at all like my sister-in-law's living room, full of those horrid Japanese screens. You've surpassed cubism, Mr. Parodi, although that's quite passé now. Still, if I were you I'd have that door given a nice coat of Duco enamel. I just love ironwork painted white. Mickey Montenegro—don't you think he's too, too divine?—told us we should come and bother you. What splendid luck to find you in! I wanted so much to speak to you personally. It's such an awful bore to have to keep repeating this story to one inspector after another. They only confuse you with a deluge of questions, and then there are my sisters-in-law, who're just too much for words.

"I'm going to tell you all about the morning of the thirtieth. There were Formento, Montenegro, Anglada, I, and my husband. Nobody else. The princess —it's a shame really that she couldn't make it, because she's just so full of *charme* which, of course, is quite extinct since the Communists. But think for a moment what feminine intuition and the maternal instinct are. When Consuelo brought me my prune juice, I had a splitting headache. Men are such brutes. The first thing I did was to go to Manuel's bedroom, but he wouldn't take any notice. He was more interested in his own headache, which wasn't nearly as awful as mine. We women, schooled as we are in motherhood, aren't so feeble. It was his fault, anyway, for having gone to bed so late. He'd been up until all hours, speaking to Formento about a book. Why in heaven he insists on talking about things he knows nothing about I'll never understand. I arrived at the tail end of their discussion, but it didn't take me long to sense what it was about. Pepe—I mean, Formento—is about to publish a popular translation of *La soirée avec M. Teste.* To reach the masses, which after all is what matters, he has called it in translation, *Once a Night with Mr. Noodle.* Manuel, who has never understood that without love charity is simply unviable, had elected to discourage Formento. He claimed that Paul Valéry recommends thinking to others but doesn't bother himself, to which Formento argued that the translation was already made, but I always say in the Casa de Arte that we ought to invite Valéry to give some lectures. I don't really know *what* was going on that day, but the wind was blowing so hot that it drove all of us nearly out of our minds—especially me, I'm so sensitive. Even nanny here forgot her place and interfered with Manuel over Pampa, who hates his gaucho costume. I can't imagine why I'm telling you these things, which actually took place the night before. On the thirtieth, after tea, Anglada, who only thinks about himself and doesn't seem to know how much I detest going for walks, insisted that I show him the water tank a second time, despite the sun and mosquitoes. Luckily, I was able to make my getaway and go back to reading Giono—now don't you dare tell me you don't like *Accompagné de la flûte.* It's a tremendous book, and it does take one's mind off the ranch. But beforehand, I wanted to see Manuel, who, with his mania for bulls, was on the terrace. It was almost six o'clock, and I climbed up the stairs to him. It was so stunning I caught my breath and said, 'Oh! What a picture!' There I was in my salmon-pink windbreaker and Vionnet shorts, leaning against the railing, and two steps away Manuel was riveted to his chair, stuck through the back of it with Pampa's toy knife. Luckily, the little angel had been out hunting cats and so was spared this horrible sight. That evening he came home with a half-dozen tails."

"They smelled so bad I had to flush them down the toilet," Miss Bilham said with almost voluptuous relish.

V

That September morning Anglada was inspired. His lucid mind embraced both past and future: the history of futurism and the plotting of certain men of letters in his behalf to get him to accept the Nobel Prize. When Parodi thought that the verbal flood had dried up, Anglada flourished a letter, saying with a kindly laugh, "Poor José! These Chilean pirates know their business, all right. Read this, Parodi, my friend. They want no truck with Formento's grotesque version of Valéry."

Acquiescing, don Isidro read:

Dear Sir,
We hasten to reaffirm what has already been explained in reply to yours of the 19th, 26th, and 30th August. It is impossible at the present time to fund the edition. Expenses for plates, for permission fees to Walt Disney, and for New Year and Easter foreign-language editions make the proposal unfeasible unless you are prepared to

pay in advance the various and sundry printing, overhead, and warehouse costs.
We remain,

Very truly yours,

(signed)
Rufino Gigena S., Assistant to the
Assistant Vice-President

"This little business note comes straight from heaven," don Isidro said, managing at last to get in a word. "Now I can begin to tie up loose ends. You've been going on and on about books for ages. Let me say a thing or two. A short time ago, I read this . . . this *thing* full of heart-warming pictures: you on stilts, you dressed as a baby, you riding your bicycle. You've no idea how I laughed! Whoever would have imagined that don Formento, a pathetic fool if ever there was one, could make you such a laughingstock! All your books are ludicrous: you bring out your *Hymns for Millionaires,* and little Sir Echo, falling over himself with respect, writes his *Odes for Managers;* you, *The Cahiers of a Cowhand* and he, *Notes of a Poultry Wholesaler.* Listen carefully now; I'm going to tell you from the beginning exactly what happened.

"First, a pompous ass came to me with a tale of the theft of a number of letters. I took no notice of him, because if someone's lost something the last person he's going to ask to find it for him is a jailbird. This same ass, maintaining that the letters compromised a lady, claimed there was nothing between the lady and him, that they were exchanging letters purely out of mutual regard. He said this to make me believe the lady was his lover. A week later, good old Montenegro turned up and said the pompous ass was beside himself with worry. This time you behaved like someone who really had lost something. You went and saw a person who hasn't landed in jail yet and who's won himself a bit of a name for criminal detection. Then everyone went off to the country, the late Muñagorri died, don Formento and a silly tramp came around bothering me, and I began to smell a rat.

"You told me your correspondence had been stolen. You even led me to believe it was Formento who'd stolen it. What you wanted was to get people talking about those letters and imagining all manner of things about you and the lady. Then the lie became reality: Formento did steal the letters. He stole them to publish them. You bored him, and after the two-hour monologue you unleashed on me this afternoon I see why. He got so fed up, in fact, that he couldn't put up with the innuendo any longer. He decided to have the correspondence published so as to finish the thing once and for all and to let the whole country know that there was nothing between you and Mariana. Muñagorri viewed things very differently. He didn't want to see his wife made a laughingstock on account of a slim volume of drivel. On the twenty-ninth, he confronted Formento. Of their discussion, Formento told me nothing. This was what they were arguing about when Mariana interrupted them, and they had the tact to make her believe they were discussing some book or other that Formento was copying from the French. What could books by people like you possibly matter to a cattle breeder? The next day, Muñagorri took Formento to El Pilar with a letter to his publishers to stop the book. To Formento this was the last straw, and he decided to get rid of Muñagorri. He had no scruples about it, because there was always the risk of his affair with the lady being discovered. That tramp simply couldn't keep her mouth shut. She went around repeating everything he said—about love and charity, about the Englishwoman who didn't know her place. Once, when she made a slip and called him by his nickname, she even managed to betray herself.

"When the boy threw away his gaucho costume, Formento saw that the moment was ripe. He was safe. He had a good alibi. He said that the door between his bedroom and the Englishwoman's was open. Neither she nor our friend Montenegro denied this. And yet, it's customary to shut a door when pastimes of that sort are going on. Formento chose the right weapon. Pampa's knife helped implicate two people—Pampa himself, who's half crazy, and you, don Anglada, who pretend to be the lady's lover just as more than once you pretended to be a child. Formento put the whip in your room for the police to find. He brought me the book with pictures of you to plant the same suspicion in me. As easy as can be, he slipped out onto the terrace and stabbed Muñagorri. The cowhands couldn't see him, because they were busy with the bulls down below.

"This is fate for you. Formento went to all that trouble to bring out a book of love letters from the tramp and some New Year greetings. You've only got to look at that woman to guess what her correspondence is like. Is it any wonder those publishing people wanted no part of it?"

Quequén,
February 22, 1942

Free Will
and the Commendatore

To the prophet Muhammad

I

The prisoner in cell 273 received Mrs. Anglada and her husband with obvious resignation.

"I'll come straight to the point and avoid circumlocution," Carlos Anglada promised solemnly. "My brain is a huge refrigerator. The circumstances of the death of Julia Ruiz Villalba—Pumita to her peers—live on in this gray vessel, untainted. I shall be scrupulously honest; I look on these matters with the detachment of a deus ex machina. I mean to offer you a cross-section of the facts. I exhort you, Parodi—be an auditory nerve."

Parodi did not lift his eyes. He went on looking at a photograph of ex-President Irigoyen. The poet's animated introduction revealed nothing new in the way of information. A few days earlier, Parodi had read an article of Molinari's on the sudden disappearance from the Argentine social scene of Miss Ruiz Villalba, one of the liveliest of the younger set.

Anglada opened his mouth to speak, but before he could, his wife Mariana took over and said, "Carlos here has dragged me to this jail when I was supposed to go to Mario's lecture on Concepción Arenal and be bored stiff. You are my rescuer, Mr. Parodi, from the Casa de Arte. Some of these so-called important figures are nothing but stuffed shirts, though I always say the Monsignor speaks with great style. Carlos, as usual, will want to put his oar in, but after all it's my sister, and they haven't dragged me all this way to keep my mouth shut like some ninny. Besides, with our native intuition we women notice things more, as Mario said when he congratulated me on my mourning costume. I was beside myself with grief, but black does look good on a bleached blonde. Look, with the luck I've been having I'm going to tell you everything from the very beginning—without a fuss and without being obsessed with books like everyone else. You probably saw in the rotogravure section that poor Pumita, my sister, was engaged to Ricky San Giacomo. Now there's a name with class, and corny though it sounds they made an ideal couple. Pumita was so pretty. She had all the style of the Ruiz Villalbas and eyes like Norma Shearer. Now that she's gone, as Mario said, mine are the only Norma Shearers left. Of course, Pumita was wild and never read anything but *Vogue,* which is why she lacked that *charme* you find in French theater, though the best you can say of Madeleine Ozeray is that she dresses like a scarecrow. Well, it's just too much all these people coming and telling me Pumita committed suicide—me, such a good Catholic since the Eucharistic Congress, and her with her joie de vivre, which I have too. After all, there's nothing mousy about me. Don't tell me this scandal is really a shame and shows a lack of consideration—as if I didn't have enough to swallow what with poor Formento sticking that little knife through the chair into Manuel, who was so gaga over his bulls. Sometimes it makes me stop and think, but then I always say what's the use?

"Ricky's famous for his super looks, but what more could he want than to marry into an old family. They're just parvenus, though the father I respect because he came to Rosario poor as a churchmouse. My sister was no fool, and Mother with her weakness for Pumita went the whole hog when she had her coming-out party, so it's no wonder she got engaged when she was only just beginning to bud. Everyone says they met in the most romantic way, in Llavalol, like Errol Flynn and Olivia de Havilland in *Vamos a Méjico,* which in English is called *Sombrero.* Pumita was out driving her tonneau, and as it reached the paved road her horse bolted. Ricardo, whose interest in life doesn't go beyond polo ponies, wanted to play Douglas Fairbanks, and he stopped her horse, which is not all that sensational. Of course, when he found out she was my sister he fell head over heels, and poor Pumita—well, she liked playing around even with the servants. The thing is that I invited Ricky out to La Moncha for her, and that was in spite of our never having met. The Commendatore—Ricky's father, you'll recall—did all he could to help things along, and Ricky was driving me absolutely crazy with the orchids he kept sending Pumita every day, so I finally got my own thing going with Bonfanti, but that's another story."

"Why don't you take a breather, madame," Parodi respectfully interrupted. "Now that the weather's cleared, don Anglada, couldn't you take the opportunity to sum things up for me?"

"Let me open fire."

"God, you're so stuffy," said Mariana, applying a careful lipstick to her disdainful mouth.

"The landscape devised by my wife is accurate.

Nonetheless, it lacks pragmatic coordinates. I shall be the surveyor, the cadastre, and embark upon a thoroughgoing synthesis.

"In Pilar, adjoining La Moncha, lay the parks, nurseries, greenhouses, observatory, gardens, swimming pool, animal cages, underground aquarium, service houses, gymnasium, and stronghold of Commendatore San Giacomo. This colorful old man—his eyes piercing, his height middling, his complexion ruddy, and his snow-white mustache cleft by a festive cheroot—is a veritable bundle of muscle on the track, the scooter, and the springboard. Now, moving from snapshot to motion picture, I'll set off without circumlocution on the life story of this fertilizer merchant. The rusty old nineteenth century went round and round, blubbering in its wheelchair—those years of the Japanese screen and madcap velocipede—when the city of Rosario opened its generous maw to an Italic immigrant. Pardon, an Italian boy. Who was that boy? I ask. Commendatore San Giacomo, I answer. Illiteracy, the Mafia, bad weather, and a blind faith in the future of the Argentine were his guides. A consular gentleman—to be exact, the Italian consul, Count Isidoro Fosco—had an inkling of the young man's moral fiber, and on several occasions offered him unselfish advice.

"In 1902, San Giacomo confronted life from the driver's seat of a Department of Sanitation cart. In 1903, he presided over a determined fleet of night-soil carts. From 1908 on—the year he got out of jail—he linked his name forever to the conversion of fats into soap. In 1910, he embraced tanning and manure. In 1914, with the eye of a Cyclops, he discerned the medicinal possibilities of asafetida, but the war destroyed this dream. Our hero, on the brink of disaster, gave

79

the rudder a sharp turn and consolidated in rhubarb. Italy was not long in putting its shoulder to the wheel. San Giacomo, from the other side of the Atlantic, shouted 'Count me in!' and dispatched a shipload of rhubarb to the latter-day trench dwellers. Not a whit discouraged by the rebelliousness of ignorant soldiers, he let his nutritive shiploads clog the docks and warehouses of Genoa, Salerno, and Castellamare, emptying more than one densely populated neighborhood. This alimentary extravagance was rewarded: the breast of the newly made millionaire was crucified with the cross and sash of a Commendatore.''

"What a way to tell a story! You're like a sleepwalker," Mariana said coolly, as she hiked up her skirt. "Before they made him Commendatore, he'd already married his cousin, whom he sent for from Italy, and you also left out anything about the children."

"I concur. I've let myself drift on the ferryboat of my verbiage. A River Plate H. G. Wells, let me row upstream in time. I shall disembark on the possessive marriage bed. Now our hero engenders his scion. A child is born. He is Ricardo San Giacomo. The mother, a barely glimpsed peripheral figure, disappears, dying in 1921. Death, who, like the postman, rings twice, deprived San Giacomo that same year of the sponsor who'd never withheld encouragement—Count Isidoro Fosco. I say, and I'll say it again without hesitation, the Commendatore veered toward madness. The crematory oven had devoured his wife's flesh. All that remained was her progeny, her likeness—her onlybegotten infant son. The father, a moral monolith, dedicated himself to educating the boy, to worshiping him. Let me stress the contradiction: the Commendatore—as hard and dictatorial among his machines as a hydraulic press—was, *chez lui,* the most pliant of his son's puppets.

"Let me throw a spotlight on this heir: gray felt hat, his mother's eyes, a circumflex mustache, the legs of an Argentine centaur, and mannerisms borrowed from the tango lyricist Juan Lomuto. This hero of poolsides and racetracks is also an attorney at law, a man of the world. I admit that his collection of poems, *Combing the Wind,* is not an iron chain of metaphors, but neither is it lacking in deep vision, in neostructural insight. Nevertheless, it's in the field of the novel where our poet will turn on all his voltage. I predict that some muscular critic is bound to point out that our iconoclast, before breaking the old molds, reproduced them; but this same critic will have to acknowledge the scientific accuracy of the copy. Ricardo is an Argentine of promise. His story of the Countess of Chinchón welds the archeological past to neofuturism. This work demands comparison with the writings of such contemporaries of his as Gandia, Levene, Grosso, and Radaelli. Happily, our explorer is not alone. Eliseo Requena, his selfless foster-brother, stands behind him and encourages his explorations. To define this acolyte I'll be as frank as a fist. Our great novelist himself deals with the central characters of his novel, leaving lesser pens to deal with lesser characters. Requena (obviously invaluable as a factotum) is one of the Commendatore's many natural sons and is neither better nor worse than the others. Or is he? He does stand out in one particular: his absolute devotion to Ricardo.

"A character of a monetary, indeed almost fiduciary complexion now comes under my lens. Stripping him of his mask, I introduce the Commendatore's financial director, Giovanni Croce. His detractors claim he's from La Rioja and that his real name is Juan Cruz. The truth is something quite different. His patriotism is obvious; his devotion to the Commendatore, constant;

81

his accent, most unpleasant. Commendatore San Giacomo, Ricardo San Giacomo, Eliseo Requena, Giovanni Croce—this is the human quartet who witnessed Pumita's last days. I leave aside in justified anonymity a whole pack of hired help: gardeners, laborers, chauffeurs, and masseurs."

Mariana could not help interrupting. "Aha! This time you can't deny you're consumed with envy and always thinking the worst of people. You haven't said a single word about Mario. His room was next to ours and was absolutely full of books. He knows a smart woman when he sees one and doesn't waste any time, but scribbles messages to her like a peacock. How he left you gaping—you couldn't even say boo! The things that man knows are incredible."

"True. I often give myself a veneer of silence. Dr. Mario Bonfanti is a Hispanist in the service of the Commendatore's household. He's published an adaptation for adults of the *Cantar de Myo Cid* and is contemplating a strict Argentinization of Gongora's *Soledades,* which he will endow with water troughs and well shafts, with sheepskin saddle blankets and nutrias."

"Don Anglada, you've made me dizzy with all those books," said Parodi. "If you want me to be of any use, tell me about your late-lamented sister-in-law. I suppose I'll hear it whether I want to or not."

"Like the critics, you don't follow me. A great painter—Picasso—places the background of his pictures in the foreground and leaves the central figure on the line of the horizon. My battle plan is the same. With the supernumeraries out of the way—Bonfanti, etc.—I attack Pumita Ruiz Villalba, corpus delicti, head on.

"The artist is never carried away by appearances. Pumita, an ephebus in her frolics, and with her slightly unkempt grace, was, above all, a backdrop. Her function was to show off my wife's opulent beauty. Pumita is dead. When I remember that function now I am unspeakably moved. It was positively Grand Guignolesque—on the night of the twenty-third of June she laughed and, warmed by my words, luxuriated in the after-dinner talk; on the twenty-fourth, she lay poisoned in her bedroom. Fate, which is no gentleman, decreed that my wife should find her."

II

On the afternoon of the twenty-third of June, the eve of her death, Pumita saw Emil Jannings die three times in scratchy but venerated copies of *High Treason, The Blue Angel,* and *The Last Command.* It was Mariana who had suggested this outing to the Pathé-Baby Club. On the way back, she and Mario Bonfanti relegated themselves to the back seat of Ricardo San Giacomo's Rollo Royce, letting Pumita ride in front with Ricky so as to complete the reconciliation, which had started in semidarkness in the movie house. Bonfanti deplored Anglada's absence. That same afternoon, the latter was at work on his *Scientific History of Moving Pictures.* He preferred to base his research on memory—his infallible artist's memory—uncontaminated by an actual viewing of the films, which is always ambiguous and misleading.

That night, in Villa Castellamare, the after-dinner talk was dialectical.

"Once again, I quote my old friend Maestro Correas," said Bonfanti eruditely. He was sporting a herringbone tweed jacket; a heavy sweater; a tartan tie; a sober, brick-colored shirt; an outsized pen and pencil set; and a referee's wrist stopwatch. "We were out for wool, and we got shorn. The spineless twits who run the Pathé-Baby Club let us down. They gave a showing of Jannings' films without putting on the best and most characteristic of them all. We've been denied the screen version of Butler's satire, *Ainsi va toute chair—The Way of All Flesh.*"

"But have we?" said Pumita. "All Jannings' films are *The Way of All Flesh.* It's the same plot every time—first they bring about his happiness, then they jinx him and bring about his downfall. It's so boring and so lifelike. I'll bet the Commendatore agrees with me."

The Commendatore hesitated. Mariana seized the opportunity and said, "I suppose it's my fault, because it was my idea that we go. You blubbered like a fool in spite of your makeup."

"That's right," Ricky said. "I saw you crying. You make yourself a nervous wreck and then you have to take those drops you keep by your bed so you can sleep at night."

"You must be the world's greatest nincompoop," Mariana said. "You know the doctor told you that stuff's bad for you. With me it's different. I'm always fighting with the servants."

"If I can't drop off straightaway my head gets filled with nagging thoughts. Never mind, it's not as if this is my last night on earth. Don't you think, Commendatore, that some people's lives are just like Jannings' pictures?"

It seemed to Ricardo that Pumita was trying to avoid the subject of insomnia. "Pumita's right," he said. "Nobody can escape his fate. Morganti was a crack polo player until the day he bought himself a piebald that brought him bad luck."

"No!" shouted the Commendatore. "No *Homo pensante* believes in bad luck. I ward it off with this rabbit's foot." And there was the foot, extracted from an inner pocket of his dinner jacket and held up in exultation.

"That's what's called a straight to the jaw," said Anglada, applauding. "Pure reason plus pure reason."

"The way I see it, there are lives in which nothing happens by chance," Pumita insisted.

"Look, if you mean me, you're out of your mind," said Mariana. "My home may be a mess, but that's because of Carlos. He's always spying on me."

"In life nothing should happen by chance," droned Croce's mournful voice. "Without discipline, without a police force, we'd fall directly into Russian chaos, into the tyranny of the Cheka. Let's face it—in the country of Ivan the Terrible, there's no longer any such thing as free will."

Visibly thoughtful, Ricardo finally said, "Things—things are what can't happen accidentally. Without order, a cow would come flying in the window."

"Even those mystics who attain the greatest heights —a Saint Teresa, a Ruysbroeck, a Blosius—hew to the imprimatur of the church, to the ecclesiastical seal of approval," Bonfanti affirmed.

The Commendatore pounded the table. "Bonfanti, I have no wish to offend you, but it's pointless for you to hide. You are, in the full sense, a Catholic. You must know that we of the Great Sunrise of the Scottish Rite dress up like priests, and we have no reason to envy any man. My blood boils when I hear it said that a man can't measure up to his fantasies."

There was an uncomfortable silence. A minute or two later, pale as death, Anglada dared mutter, "A TKO. The first line of the determinists has been smashed. We're filling the breach; they flee in complete disorder. As far as the eye can see, the battlefield is littered with weapons and baggage."

"Don't pretend you won that argument, because it wasn't you. You were tongue-tied," said Mariana mercilessly.

"Just think," Pumita said absentmindedly, "everything we say will find its way into the notebook that the Commendatore brought from Salerno."

"And what does our friend Eliseo Requena have to say?" asked Croce, the gloomy administrator, trying to change the subject.

Requena, a huge young albino, answered in a mousy voice. "I'm a very busy man—Ricky's about to finish his novel."

Ricky blushed and clarified: "I work like a mole, but Pumita advises me to take my time."

"If I were you, I'd put the draft away in a drawer and forget about it for nine years," said Pumita.

"Nine years?" exclaimed the Commendatore, on the brink of an apoplectic fit. "Nine years? Dante published the *Divine Comedy* five hundred years ago."

Nobly, Bonfanti rushed to the aid of the Commendatore. "Hear, hear," he said. "Such hesitation is Nordic, worthy of a Hamlet. The Roman concept of art was altogether different. To them, writing was a harmonious act, a dance, not the gloomy discipline of the barbarian, who tries with monkish mortification to supply the salt that Minerva denies him."

The Commendatore grew insistent. "He who does not put down in writing the ferment in his head is a eunuch of the Sistine Chapel. He is not a man."

"I, too, am of the opinion that the writer must give wholly of himself," said Requena. "Contradictions don't matter. The thing is to spill out onto paper all the muddle and confusion which is the human condition."

"When I write my mother if I once stop to think I can't think of anything," Mariana interrupted. "But if I let myself go it's marvelous. I fill pages and pages without even realizing it. You yourself, Carlos, assured me that I was born to write."

"Look, Ricky," Pumita insisted, "if I were you I wouldn't listen to any advice but mine. You can't be too careful about what you publish. Remember Bustos Domecq, that man from Santa Fe who got a story published and then it turned out that it had already been written by Villiers de l'Isle Adam?"

"We made up only two hours ago," Ricky snapped at her, "and there you go again."

"Calm down, Pumita," said Requena. "Ricky's novel is nothing like Villiers'."

"You don't understand me, Rick. I'm doing this for your own good. I'm very nervous tonight, but tomorrow we'll have a long talk."

Bonfanti wanted to win a victory. "Ricky's too sensible to surrender to mere trendiness, which has no native Hispanic roots," he pontificated. "The writer who does not feel the message of his blood and birthplace rising in his sap is *déraciné,* an outcast."

"I hardly recognize you, Mario," said the Commendatore with approval. "This time you haven't played the jester. True art is born of the earth. It's a verifiable law. I have the noblest Maddaloni tucked away in my cellars. Throughout Europe and even America they're stashing away the works of the great masters in bombproof cellars. Last week a reputable archeologist showed me a terra-cotta puma that he had in his suitcase and that he'd dug up in Peru. He let me have it at cost, and now I keep it in the third drawer of my private desk."

"A little puma?" Pumita said with surprise.

"That's right," said Anglada. "The Aztecs had a premonition about you. Let's not demand too much of them. Futuristic as they may have been, they could never have imagined Mariana's functional beauty."

(It was with a fair degree of accuracy that Carlos Anglada relayed this conversation to Parodi.)

III

On the following Friday, first thing in the morning, Ricardo San Giacomo was talking to don Isidro. The sincerity of his grief was obvious. He was pale, in mourning clothes, and unshaven. He said he hadn't slept that night, nor had he got any sleep for several nights.

"It's awful what's happening to me," he said gloomily. "It's really awful. You, sir, who have been leading a more or less normal life, from rooming house to jail, so to speak, can't begin to imagine what this means to me. I've been around, but I've never had any trouble I couldn't smooth over at once. For example, when one of the Dolly sisters came to me with a story of her natural child, my old man, who looks like somebody incapable of understanding these things, took care of her instantly with six thousand pesos. Besides, it's fairly obvious that I know how to look after myself. Some time ago, over in Montevideo, the roulette table cleaned me out of my last cent. It was tremendous. Guys were sweating just watching me play. In under twenty minutes I lost twenty thousand pesos. Look at the fix I was in. I didn't even have the change to phone

Buenos Aires. Still, cool as can be, I strolled out onto the terrace. Would you believe that I solved the problem on the spot? Out of the blue steps this little character who talks through his nose and who's been following my game closely. He lends me five thousand pesos. The next day I was back at Villa Castellamare, having won back five thousand pesos of the twenty thousand that the Uruguayans had nicked me for. The little guy never saw me again.

"As for running around with women, don't let me get started on that. If you want some fun, just ask Mickey Montenegro what sort of cat I am. I'm the same in everything. Find out how I study; I don't even open the books. When exams come around I crack a joke or two, and the examiners congratulate me. Now, to help me get over this bad experience with Pumita, the old man wants me to go into politics. Dr. Saponaro, who's clever as a fox, says he isn't sure yet which political party suits me best. But I'll bet you anything you like that next half-time I'll be running for Congress. It's the same in polo. Who's got the best ponies? Who's the crack player in Tortuga Park? I'll stop before I bore you.

"I don't talk hot air like la Barcina, who was going to be my sister-in-law, or like her husband, who's always talking about soccer when he's never laid eyes on a regulation ball. I want you to start getting clued in. I was about to marry Pumita. Sure, she had her downs, but she was really wonderful. Overnight, she's poisoned with cyanide—dead, to put it bluntly. First they let it out that she committed suicide. That's crazy, because we were about to get married. You can be sure I wasn't going to give my name to some suicidal nut. Then they said she took the poison by mistake— as if she didn't have a brain in her head. Now they come out with something new—murder—which casts a shadow over us all. What do you want me to say? Between murder and suicide, I'll take suicide, even though that's a load of rubbish."

"Look here, young man," said Parodi, "with all this talk this cell's just like an election rostrum. As soon as I'm not looking, some clown slips in here with a tale about signs of the Zodiac, or about a train that doesn't stop anywhere, or about a fiancée who never committed suicide, who never drank poison by mistake, and who never got murdered. I'm going to order Assistant Chief Grondona to clap the whole lot in the clink the next time he as much as catches a glimpse of them."

"But I'm here to help you, Mr. Parodi. That is to say, I want to ask you to help me."

"All right. That's the way I like a man. Let's see. Can we take it step by step now? Are you sure the deceased could stomach the idea of marrying you?"

"As sure as I'm my father's son. Pumita had her moods, but she loved me."

"Pay attention to my questions. Was she pregnant? Was she playing around with some other fool? Did she need money? Was she ill? Was she beginning to bore you?"

After thinking awhile, San Giacomo answered in the negative.

"Now explain to me this thing about the sleeping medicine."

"Well, Dr. Parodi, we didn't like her taking it. But she kept on buying it, and she hid it in her room."

"Did you have access to that room? Did anybody else?"

"Anyone could have got in," the young man said. "All the bedrooms of that wing look out onto the circular lawn with its row of statues."

On the nineteenth of July, Mario Bonfanti burst into cell 273. Swiftly shedding his white mackintosh and doeskin trilby, he tossed his malacca cane onto the regulation cot, pulled out a cigarette lighter and lit a new meerschaum pipe. Then, taking an oblong piece of mustard-colored chamois out of a secret pocket, he vigorously wiped the lenses of his dark glasses. For a minute or two, his iridescent scarf and thick woolen waistcoat heaved under his audible breathing. Through the pipestem between his teeth, his fresh Italian voice, embellished with a Castilian lisp, sounded seductive and forceful.

"Maestro Parodi, I'm sure you know how the police operate—their style. Personally, I have to admit that, inclined as I am more to scholarship than to the intricacies of criminal investigation, all this took me by surprise. In short, here are the cops, absolutely convinced that Pumita's suicide was a murder. The fact is that these back-room Edgar Wallaces have me under suspicion. Clearly, I'm forward-looking, a progressive. Some days ago, I deemed it wise to make a gracious perusal of certain love letters. I wanted to cleanse my mind, to unburden myself of all sentimental ballast. It's superfluous to reveal the lady's name. Neither you nor I, Isidro Parodi, have any interest in mere surnames. Thanks to this *briquet,* if you'll permit the Gallicism," Bonfanti added, brandishing his outsized cigarette lighter in triumph, "I made a conclusive epistolary pyre in the fireplace of my bedroom-study. Then look what happened. The bloodhounds made a great fuss about it. That innocent bonfire got me a weekend in jail, a harsh exile from the comforts of home and from my accustomed daily newspaper. Of course, deep down inside I soared above it all. But now I've returned to earth. I can't help thinking I'm going to meet up with these ugly brutes again. I ask you in all sincerity, do you consider me to be in danger?"

"Yes, of going on and on until Doomsday," answered Parodi. "If you don't relax, you'll be taken for a Spaniard. Pretend you aren't drunk and tell me what you know about the death of Ricky San Giacomo."

"All my expository abilities, my whole verbal cornucopia, are at your disposal. In a jiffy, I'll sketch you an outline of the case in broad strokes. I shall not try to conceal from your perspicacious intellect, my dear Parodi, that Pumita's death had affected Ricky—not to say shattered him. Doña Mariana Ruiz Villalba de Anglada is by no means crazy when she declares, with that enviable grace of hers, that polo ponies are Ricardo's be-all and end-all. Imagine our great surprise when we learned that, embittered and pining away, he had sold off those superb stables of his. Only yesterday they had been the apple of his eye and now he looked upon them without joy, without love. He was no longer wining and dining. Not even the publication of his novel, *The Sword at Noon,* whose manuscript I personally spiced up for the press, raised his spirits. You, as an old hand at literary detection, will not have failed to notice and to applaud more than one trace of my highly personal style—each trace, I might add, the size of an ostrich egg. Now we're getting down to one of the Commendatore's kindly acts, to one of his long-standing schemes. In order to bring his son's melancholy to an end, the father secretly speeded up the printing of the book and like greased lightning he surprised Ricky with six hundred and fifty copies on Wathman paper, in Teufelsbible format. On the q.t., the Commendatore is like Proteus. He consults top doctors; he confers with his bank's straw men; he refuses to contribute a farthing to the Baroness de Servus, who wields the peremptory scepter of the Anti-Semitic Relief Society. He divides his wealth in two parts, the larger, destined for his legitimate son —millions upon millions, which will triple in five years —he sinks into the new underground rapid transit system. The smaller part, slumbering in meager share certificates, he leaves to Eliseo Requena, his son fathered on the field of love. The Commendatore does all this while managing to postpone my fees indefinitely and to fall out with the manager of the print shop, an old debtor of his.

"A compliment is better than the truth. A week after the publication of *The Sword at Noon,* don José María Pemán wrote a tribute to it. Doubtless he was attracted to the book by certain ornaments and adornments that were obvious to any intelligent mind and that also stood out from Requena's sledgehammer syntax and feeble vocabulary. Fortune smiled on Ricky, but he became both boring and inconsiderate, and persisted in his pointless mourning of Pumita. I can already hear you muttering to yourself, 'Let the dead bury the dead.' Without engaging in any sterile argument about the point of that remark, let me say that I myself suggested to Ricardo the need, what's more the advisability, of burying his present grief and seeking comfort in the bountiful wellsprings of the past, which is the arsenal and festive board of all new shoots. I advised him to revive some little peccadillo that predated Pumita's arrival on the scene. Good advice is half the battle. No sooner said than done. In no time at all, our Ricardo, revived and in good spirits, was piloting the elevator up to the residence of the Baroness de Servus. See that? I'm a top-flight reporter, and I'm not withholding genuine information—her actual name. History, moreover, reveals refined primitivism to be the undeniably exclusive possession of the Teutonic grande dame. The first act glides onto an aquatic, amphibious stage during that sultry spring of 1937. Through nonchalant binoculars our Ricardo was spying on the heats of a women's sculling regatta—the Valkyries of Ruderverein versus the Columbines of Neptunia. All at once the intruding glass comes to rest; Ricardo gapes; thirstily he takes in the trim, graceful figure of Baroness de Servus, riding her clinker-built craft. That same evening, an old copy of the *Tatler* was mutilated; that night a picture of the baroness, set off by her faithful Doberman pinscher, presided over the young man's insomnia. 'Some wacky Frenchwoman is pestering me with phone calls,' Ricardo told me a week later. 'To make her stop, I'm going to see her.' As you see, I'm repeating the very words of our conversation. Let me sketch the first night of love. Ricardo arrives at the aforesaid residence. He goes up, vertically, in the elevator. He is escorted into an intimate sitting room. He is left alone; suddenly the light goes out. Two possibilities tug at the young man's mind: a short circuit and a kidnapping. First he sobs, then he whimpers, then he curses the day he was born. At last he stretches out his arms. A weary voice entreats him gently but firmly. The dark is pleasant and the sofa inviting. Dawn, the eternal woman, restores his sight. I can no longer hold it back, my dear friend Parodi: Ricardo awoke in the arms of the Baroness de Servus.

"Your life and mine, more sedentary, perhaps more reflective, can do without this sort of thing. But Ricardo couldn't.

"Trying to come to terms with Pumita's death, he seeks out the baroness. Our Gregorio Martínez Sierra was harsh but just when he coined the phrase 'Woman is the contemporary sphinx.' Of course, you won't ask me as a gentleman to reveal word for word the conversation that took place between this unpredictable grande dame and her importunate lover, who wanted a shoulder to cry on. These cosy little chats, these tidbits of gossip, are better suited to coarse, Frenchified novelists, not to seekers after truth. Besides, I have no idea what they talked about. The fact is that half an hour later, shaken and crestfallen, Ricardo came down in the same Otis elevator which on previous occasions had lifted him upward, so sure of himself. Here is where the tragic dance begins. You're losing yourself, Ricardo, you're going over the edge! Careful, because you're already sliding into the abyss of madness! I shan't withhold from you a single station of this incomprehensible *via crucis*. After speaking to the baroness, Ricardo went to Miss Dollie Vavasour's house. She was a third-rate touring actress who had no ties and who I know had had an affair with him. You'll be annoyed, Parodi, if I dwell on, if I enlarge upon, this cheap slut. One stroke is enough to paint her life-size. I once paid her the compliment of sending her a copy of my *Góngora Has Already Said It All,* enhanced by a dedication in my own hand and by my holograph signature. The rude woman never acknowledged the gift in spite of my efforts to entice her with offerings of chocolates, pastries, and sweet drinks, together with which I included my *Research into Aragonisms in Some Pamphlets by J. Cejador y Frauca,* in a deluxe edition, which I conveyed to her private residence by the Grand Splendid Messenger Service.

"I keep scouring my brain, asking myself over and over what aberration, what moral bankruptcy, induced

Ricardo to direct his steps to that den, which I am proud never to have entered and which is a well-known public dispensary for all kinds of sensual gratification. The punishment lies in the sin. After a bleak conversation with this Englishwoman, Ricardo left hurriedly and thoroughly depressed, swallowing over and over again the bitter fruit of his disillusion. The wings of insanity beat at his jaunty hat. Not far from the Englishwoman's house—at the corner of Juncal and Esmeralda, to add a dash of local color—he took himself boldly in hand. He quickly boarded a taxi which eventually deposited him at the doorstep of a family boardinghouse in the 900 block of Maipú Street. A wind filled his sails. In that safe refuge—ignored by the crowds of passersby, who are motorized thanks to the almighty dollar—lived and still lives Miss Amy Evans. Miss Evans is a woman who, without renouncing her femininity, shuffles horizons and sniffs out climates or, in a word, works for an inter-American firm whose local head is Gervasio Montenegro and whose praiseworthy purpose is to foster the emigration of the South American woman—'our Latin sister,' as Miss Evans graciously puts it—to Salt Lake City and the green farms round about. Miss Evans' time is priceless. Nonetheless, this lady stole a *mauvais quart d'heure* from the pressures of the mail and with complete dignity received the friend who, following the trauma of a broken engagement, had once escaped her advances. Ten minutes of small talk with Miss Evans are quite enough to invigorate the feeblest mind.* Ricardo, poor fellow, made it to the elevator with his spirits dragging and with the word suicide

*Mario is sometimes so aggressive. [Footnote contributed by Doña Mariana Ruiz Villalba de Anglada.]

clearly etched in his eyes. Clear, that is, to anyone with a seer's patience to decipher it.

"In times of black melancholy there's no medicine like simple daily contact with nature, which, heedful of the lure of April, breaks out in summery profusion over the hills and plains. Broken by adversity, Ricardo sought rural solitude, heading straight for suburban Avellaneda. The old mansion of the Montenegros opened its heavily curtained French doors to receive him. The host, who in matters of hospitality is every inch a man's man, accepted an extra-long Corona and, between puffs, spoke like an oracle. He revealed so much that our Ricardo, downhearted and disgruntled, was obliged to retreat to Villa Castellamare as if in flight from twenty thousand of the world's most hideous devils.

"The gloomy antechambers of madness are the waiting rooms of suicide. That night Ricardo spoke to no one who might have lifted his spirits, neither comrade nor fellow-writer. Instead, he sank into the first of a long series of conferences with the decrepit Croce, who was drier and duller than the figures in his account books.

"Our Ricardo wasted three days on those morbid discussions. On Friday, he returned to his senses, appearing of his own free will in my bedroom-study. To disinfect his soul, I invited him to correct the proof-sheets of my new edition of Rodó's *Ariel,* a masterpiece which in González Blanco's opinion 'outdoes Valera in versatility, Pérez Galdós in elegance, Pardo Bazán in refinement, Pereda in modernity, Valle Inclán in didacticism, and Azorín in critical spirit.' I suspect that anyone else would have prescribed a placebo for Ricardo rather than the lion marrow that I suggested. Nonetheless, only a minute or two of this riveting work were enough for the deceased to take his leave, comforted and at ease. I hadn't quite put on my spectacles to continue my work when, from the other side of the circular lawn, the fatal shot rang out.

"Outside, I met Requena. Ricardo's bedroom door was half shut. On the ground, sullying a soft blanket with its doomed blood, the body lay face up. Still warm, the revolver watched over Ricardo's eternal sleep.

"I'll say this openly. The decision was premeditated. This is proved and confirmed by the sad suicide note he left us. It was deficient, as if written by someone ignorant of the resources of the language; poor, as if by a bungler who has no stock of adjectives at his disposal; insipid, as if by someone unaccustomed to playing with words. It clearly shows what I have more than once maintained from the podium: that the graduates of our so-called schools are unfamiliar with the mysteries of the dictionary. Let me read it to you. You'll be the most ardent warrior in this crusade for better expression."

This is the letter that Bonfanti read only moments before don Isidro threw him out:

> The worst of it is that I have always been happy. Now everything has changed and will go on changing. I am taking my life because I no longer understand anything. My whole life has been a lie. I can't say goodbye to Pumita because she's already dead. No other father in the world has done what my father has. I want everyone to know this. Goodbye and forget me.
>
> (signed)
> Ricardo San Giacomo,
> Pilar, 11 July 1941

V

Shortly after, Parodi received a visit from Dr. Bernardo Castillo, the San Giacomo family doctor. Their conversation was long and confidential. The same can be said about the conversation that don Isidro had around that same time with the accountant Giovanni Croce.

VI

One year later, on Friday, the seventeenth of July, 1942, Mario Bonfanti—wearing a loose-fitting mackintosh, a battered trilby, a pale tartan tie, and a brand-new red sweatshirt—made a flustered entry into cell 273. He was encumbered by a vast serving platter covered with a spotless napkin.

"Fuel for the stomach!" he shouted. "Before I can count up to one on my finger, you'll be licking yours, Parodi, my charming friend. Pancakes and honey! These meat pasties were baked by honest hands. The tray that bears them boasts the princess's coat of arms and motto *Hic jacet.*"

A malacca cane checked him. It was brandished by that third musketeer, Gervasio Montenegro, who was dressed in a Houdin opera hat, a Chamberlain monocle, a sentimental black mustache, an overcoat with mink collar and cuffs, a stiff collar with a single Mendax pearl, footwear by Nimbo, and gloves by Bulpington. "I'm so glad to find you in, my dear Parodi," he exclaimed elegantly. "Please excuse my secretary's *fadaise.* We mustn't let ourselves be put off by the sophisms of Ciudadela and San Fernando streets.

99

Every thinking man knows that Avellaneda ranks first on its own merits. I never tire of telling Bonfanti that his little aphorisms and archaisms are distinctly *vieux jeu,* out of place. I guide his reading in vain. A strict regimen of Anatole France, Oscar Wilde, Toulet, don Juan Valera, Fradique Mendes, and Roberto Gache has not penetrated his intractable mind. Bonfanti, don't be stubborn and *révolté* and put down at once the pasty you've just taken, then get yourself to the Full-Blown Rose, the plumber's, at 5791 Costa Rica Street, and see if you can't make yourself useful."

Bonfanti murmured the words "Right away, sir," and bowing and scraping he made a dignified exit.

"You, don Montenegro, who are riding a tame horse," said Parodi, "be so kind as to open that air-shaft lest we be overcome by the smell of these little pasties, which must have been cooked in lard."

Swift as a duelist, Montenegro climbed up onto a stool and obeyed the master's order. He descended with a theatrical leap. "Well," he said, staring at a stubbed-out cigarette, "the time has come around at last." Drawing out a big gold watch, he wound it up and then consulted it. "Today's the seventeenth of July. It's exactly one year ago that you solved the cruel puzzle of Villa Castellamare. In this friendly atmosphere, I raise my glass and remind you that you promised me then that on this date, a year to the day, you would give a complete explanation of the mystery. I must tell you, dear Parodi, that as a dreamer, in moments stolen from my business affairs and my writings, I have come up with a quite interesting and original theory. With your disciplined mind, you may be able to contribute something useful to this theory, to this lofty intellectual edifice. I am a free-form architect. I hold out my hand for your valuable grain of sand, reserving—*cela va sans dire*—the right to reject anything too unsound or fantastic."

"Don't worry," said Parodi. "Your grain of sand will turn out to be the same as mine—especially if I speak before you do. You start, friend Montenegro. The first fruits go to the birds."

"By no means," Montenegro hastened to reply. *"Après vous, messieurs les anglais.* Besides, I can't pretend that my interest hasn't almost evaporated. The Commendatore disappointed me. I considered him a man of greater substance. He died—prepare yourself for a strong metaphor—on his uppers. The disposal of his estate barely covered his debts. I don't argue that Requena's position isn't enviable and that the huge Hamburg oratory and pair of live tapirs I bought in the auction for a ridiculous price haven't given me a good deal of pleasure. The princess can't complain either. She has rescued from foreign riffraff a terra-cotta serpent, a *fouille* from Peru which the Commendatore once cherished and kept in a drawer of his private desk and which now, rich with mythological overtones, presides over our waiting room. *Pardon.* On a previous visit I told you about this disturbing ophidian. Man of taste that I am, I had kept a place *in petto* for a writhing bronze by Boccioni, a suggestive, dynamic monster that I had to do without, because dear Mariana—I mean, Mrs. Anglada—already had her eye on it, and I chose an honorable retreat. This gambit has been rewarded. The climate of our relationship is now distinctly warm. But I digress and lead you astray, my dear Parodi. I eagerly await your summation, and in advance let me offer a word of encouragement. I speak to you proudly. No doubt what I've just said would bring a smile to the lips of more than one evil-minded person, but you know that my words are backed by solid credit. I have carried out my part of the bargain. I've sketched you a *raccourci* of my efforts with the Baroness de Servus, Lola Vicuña de Kruif, and that distracting *fausse maigre,* Dolores Vavasour. By setting up a mélange of subterfuges and threats, I managed to have Giovanni Croce, that true Cato of accountants, jeopardize his reputation by paying a visit to this penal institution only a short while before he fled the country. I've put at your service no less than one copy of that viperous pamphlet which inundated Buenos Aires and its environs, and whose author, shielded by a mask of anonymity and standing before the still-unsealed cenotaph, made himself thoroughly ridiculous by alleging that there were all kinds of absurd similarities between Ricardo's novel and Pemán's *Santa Virreina,* a work that his literary mentors, Eliseo Requena and Mario Bonfanti, chose as their strict model. This pamphleteer showed that Ricardo's little opus, despite poaching a few chapters of Pemán's potboiler—a quite innocent coincidence in the early ferment of inspiration—should have been considered rather a copy of Paul Groussac's *Billete de lotería,* reset in the seventeenth century and esteemed for its continual reminders of the sensational discovery of the tonic properties of quinine.

"*Parlons d'autre chose.* Attentive to your senile whims, my dear Parodi, I've arranged for Dr. Castillo, the brown bread and gruel fanatic, to leave his hydropathic clinic for a moment and examine you with a professional eye."

"Stop playing the fool," said the criminologist. "The San Giacomo maze has more turns to it than a clock. I began tying up loose ends on the afternoon that don Anglada and Mrs. Barcina told me about the argument at the Commendatore's on the eve of the first death. What I was later told by the late Ricardo, by Mario Bonfanti, and by you, the accountant, and the doctor confirmed my suspicions. Even the letter that the poor boy left explained everything. As Ernesto Poncio used to say,

'Fate, in its tidiness,
ties off every stitch.'

"Even old San Giacomo's death and that pamphlet written under the cover of anonymity help unravel the mystery. If I didn't know don Anglada, I'd suspect that he was beginning to see the light. The proof is that in order to tell us about Pumita's death he went all the way back to old man San Giacomo's arrival in Rosario. God speaks through the mouths of fools. That time and place is where the story really begins. The police, who always stick to what's under their noses, discovered nothing, because they were thinking about Pumita and Villa Castellamare and the year 1941. But being so long behind bars I have turned historian, and I like looking back on those days when one was young and hadn't yet been sent to jail and always had a little spending money. The story, as I say, goes a long way back, and the Commendatore is the key. Let's size up this greenhorn. In 1921, according to Anglada, he nearly went crazy. Let's see what had happened to him. His immigrant wife, whom he had sent for from Italy, died. He barely knew her. Do you imagine a man like the Commendatore is going to go crazy over that? Step aside, I'm going to spit. Again according to Anglada, the death of his friend Count Isidoro Fosco also kept him awake nights. This I don't believe, even if the *Almanac* swore to it. The count was a millionaire, a consul, and when San Giacomo was a garbage collector the count gave him nothing more than advice. The death of a friend like that is more of a relief, unless you're looking for misery. Even in business San Giacomo did well. The entire Italian army gagged on his rhubarb, which he sold them at the price of real food and for which he was even made a Commendatore. So what was the matter with him? The same old story, my friend. The Italian girl played him dirty with Count Fosco. What was worse, when San Giacomo found out about it the two sly ones were already dead.

"You know how revengeful and even bitter the Calabrians are. Worse than clerks from the Eighth Precinct. Since he couldn't avenge himself on the woman or on the hypocrite who kept giving him advice, the Commendatore avenged himself on their son —on Ricardo.

"Anybody else—you, for example—out to avenge yourself, would have been a bit hard on the alleged son and that would have been the end of it. But old San Giacomo became wild with hate. He concocted a plan which even ex-President Mitre would never have thought of. For a fine piece of long-range planning, you really have to take your hat off to the man. He mapped out Ricardo's whole life, allotting the first twenty years to his happiness and the next twenty to his downfall. However fantastic this may seem, nothing in Ricardo's life happened by chance.

"Let's start by what you know all about—women. We have the Baroness de Servus, the sister, Dolores, and Vicuña. Every one of these affairs had been prearranged by the old man without Ricardo's suspecting it. No need to tell you about this, don Montenegro, as I'm sure that with your cut you've grown sleek as a fatted calf. Even meeting Pumita seems more rigged than a Rioja election. The same goes for his law-school exams. Ricardo made no effort, yet good grades just poured in. The same thing was about to happen to him in politics. With Saponaro in the driver's seat, everybody makes it. Look, it's a real laugh—it was always the same story. Remember the six thousand pesos to buy off the Dolly sister? Remember the little guy who talked through his nose who suddenly popped up in Montevideo? He worked for San Giacomo. The proof is that he made no attempt to get back the five thousand Uruguayan pesos he lent Ricardo. And then take the case of the novel. You said yourself just now that Requena and Mario Bonfanti acted as Ricardo's front men. On the eve of Pumita's death, Requena himself let it slip, saying he was very busy because Ricardo was finishing his novel. He couldn't have made it clearer—the one who was actually writing the book was Requena. Then Bonfanti came along and puffed it up to the size of an ostrich egg.

"And so we come to the year 1941. Ricardo thought he was acting of his own free will, like any of us, but the fact is that he was being manipulated like a chess piece. They got him engaged to Pumita, who, however you look at it, came from a good family. Everything went smoothly until the father, who'd had the arrogance to think he could play God, discovered that God had been manipulating him. His health deteriorated. Dr. Castillo told him he had barely a year to live. As to what was actually wrong with him the doctor can say what he likes. Personally, I think he had a coronary. San Giacomo speeded up the dance. He had only one year left in which to pile on the last of the happiness and all the misery and disaster. The prospect did not daunt him. But during dinner on the twenty-third of

June, Pumita let him know that she had discovered the plot. Of course, she never actually told him so. They were not alone. She spoke only about movies. She said of a certain Juárez that first they piled on the triumphs and then they turned his luck against him. San Giacomo wanted to change the subject, but Pumita insisted on repeating that in some people's lives nothing happens by chance. She also brought up the subject of the notebook in which the old man kept his diary. She did this to let him know that she'd read it. In order to be sure, San Giacomo set a trap for her. He talked about a ceramic lizard that a Jew had sold him out of a suitcase and that he kept in his desk in the same drawer as the notebook. He lied that the lizard was a lion. Pumita, who knew it was a snake, was taken aback. Out of sheer jealousy, she'd been searching the old man's desk drawers looking for Ricardo's letters. She found the diary, and as she was in a studious mood she read it and discovered the plot. That night during the dinner conversation she was extremely careless. The most dangerous thing she said was that the next day she was going to talk to Ricardo. The old man, to salvage the plan he had devised with such painstaking hatred, decided to kill Pumita. He put poison in her sleeping medicine. You may remember that Ricardo had mentioned that the medicine was in her chest of drawers. It wasn't hard getting into her bedroom. All the rooms opened onto the corridor with the statues.

"Let me turn to other aspects of that night's conversation. The girl asked Ricardo to withhold publication of his so-called novel for a few years. San Giacomo openly disagreed. He wanted the book to appear so as to be able to distribute a pamphlet demonstrating that the novel was a complete plagiarism. In my opinion, the pamphlet was written by Anglada when he said he was staying home to write a history of the movies. At the same time, he announced that somebody in the know was going to see that Ricardo's novel was copied.

"As the law didn't allow San Giacomo to disinherit Ricardo, the Commendatore chose to lose his fortune. Requena's share he put into government bonds, which although not very profitable were safe. Ricardo's portion he invested in the subway. You only had to see the interest it earned to realize it was a risky investment. Croce robbed him left and right. The Commendatore let him get away with it so as to be quite sure that Ricardo would never get a bean.

"It wasn't long before money began to grow scarce. Bonfanti was cut off the payroll. The baroness was sent packing. Ricardo had to sell his polo ponies.

"The poor guy! He'd never been down before. To lift his spirits he went to see the baroness. She, angry to have got nothing out of the affair, left him flat and swore that if she'd ever had any relationship with him it was because his father was paying her. Ricardo saw his luck change, but he couldn't understand it. In his confusion he had a premonition. He went to question the Dolly sister and the Evans woman. Both of them admitted that if they'd had anything to do with him in the past it was because of an agreement they had with his father. Then he went to see you, Montenegro. You admitted that you had fixed things with those women and others. Isn't that so?"

"Unto Caesar what is Caesar's," Montenegro declared, feigning a yawn. "I'm sure you know that the orchestration of those *ententes cordiales* has by now become second nature to me."

"Worried by his lack of money, Ricardo consulted Croce. Their conversation proved that the Commendatore was deliberately ruining himself.

"The realization that his whole life was a farce both bewildered and humiliated Ricardo. It was as if suddenly you'd been told you were someone else. Ricardo had always thought a lot of himself. Now he saw that his past and all his successes had been staged by his father, and that his father, for some reason or other, was his enemy and was preparing a living hell for him. This was what made Ricardo think that life wasn't worth living. He never complained, he never said a thing against the Commendatore, whom he still loved. But he left a farewell letter that his father was sure to understand. That letter said, 'Now everything has changed and will go on changing. . . . No other father in the world has done what my father has.'

"Maybe it's because I've been living in this establishment for so long that I no longer believe in punishment. Everyone finds punishment enough in his own wrongdoing. It's not right that honest men be other men's executioners. The Commendatore had only a few months to live. Why spoil them by informing on him and pointlessly stirring up a hornet's nest of lawyers, judges, and police chiefs?"

Pujato,
August 4, 1942

Tadeo Limardo's Victim

To the memory of Franz Kafka

I

The convict in cell 273, don Isidro Parodi, received his visitor with a certain reluctance. Another hoodlum come to pester me, he thought. Parodi was unaware that twenty years earlier, before he had become an old established Argentine, he used to speak exactly like this man, drawing out his s's and waving his arms about.

Savastano straightened his tie and tossed his brown hat onto the regulation cot. He was dark, good-looking, and slightly unpleasant.

"It was Mr. Molinari who said I should trouble you," he explained. "I've come about the murder at the New Impartial Hotel—the mystery that's baffled all the top brains. Please understand. I'm here as a disinterested party, but the police have their eyes on me, and I've heard that for solving a riddle there's nobody like you. Let me tell you the facts *grosso modo* and quite frankly. That's the kind of man I am.

"The ups and downs of life have forced me, for a while, to mark time. Right now I'm in the clear, just sitting back and waiting to see how things turn out. I don't get worked up about nothing. A man sizes things up, keeps cool, and, when the time's right, he strikes. You'll never believe me when I tell you I haven't been anywhere near the Wholesale Market for a full year now. When they see me, the boys are going to say, 'Who is this guy?' I bet you anything their mouths will fall open when I show up in my little pickup. But for the time being I've retired to winter quarters. To be perfectly frank, to the New Impartial Hotel, in the 3400 block of Cangallo Street—a nook of Buenos Aires that has its own particular flavor. Personally, it's not really my choice that I live in this part of town, and one of these fine days,

'I'll beat a hasty retreat,
whistling a waltz that's slow and sweet.'

"Those lured by the sign in the doorway saying 'Beds for Gentlemen from 60-Cents Up' get the idea that the place is some sort of fleabag. But please, don't let that fool you, don Isidro. I myself have my own private room that I temporarily share with Simon Fineberg, commonly known as the Great Profile, but he's always at the Catechist's Club. Fineberg's one of those birds of passage who turn up in Merlo one day and in Berazategui the next, and he was already occupying the room when I arrived there two years ago, and I don't expect he'll ever move out. I'm speaking to you with my hand on my heart. Stick-in-the-muds get on my nerves. We're not in the oxcart age, and I'm one of those travelers who like a change of scene. And now to the point. Fineberg's a bit out of his element. He thinks the world moves around his locked trunk, but when you're broke do you think he'll let an Argentine have a couple of pesos? The rest of the boys enjoy themselves—it's a real laugh a minute—while all a zombie like Fineberg gets is a sneer.

"You, here in your niche, in your lookout post, so to speak, will like the circus I'm about to present to you. The New Impartial has an atmosphere that would arouse the interest of any student of life. It's a freak show that'll make you split a gut. I'm always saying to Fineberg, 'Why blow good money on Chaplin when we've got our own zoo right here?' To be quite frank, his features give him away. He looks like a speckled egg with ginger hair. It's no wonder that Juana Musante gave him the brushoff. This Musante woman, you see, inasmuch as she's Claudio Zarlenga's mistress, is more or less the landlady. Mr. Vicente Renovales and the aforementioned Zarlenga are the pair who run the place. Three years ago, Renovales took Zarlenga in as a partner. The old man was tired of struggling on his own, and this injection of young blood gave the New Impartial a new lease on life. Between you and me, I'll tell you something that's an open secret. Things are worse now than before, and business is only a ghost of what it used to be.

"Coming as he did from the Province of La Pampa, Zarlenga's arrival on the scene was a fateful event. I have an idea he's on the lam. Work it out for yourself. Zarlenga had taken Musante away from a post office clerk back in Banderaló. This drain on the national budget, who was something of a strongarm man, was left with his mouth hanging open. Zarlenga, who knows that down in La Pampa people don't play around with things like that, grabbed the first train and made his way here to Buenos Aires. He came to lose himself in the crowd, if you get my meaning. As for me, I didn't need even a crosstown bus to make myself invisible. From dawn to dusk I spend the whole day burrowed in my room, which is just a hole in the wall. I have to chuckle at Meat Juice's gang, swaggering up and down the Wholesale Market and never so much as seeing hide nor hair of me. To be on the safe side, I once passed them on the bus and made a face so I'd be taken for someone else.

"Zarlenga is an animal with clothes on, uncouth, a big hood—no offense meant. I may as well admit it— he treats me with kid gloves. The only time he raised a hand to me was one time when he was drinking, and because it was my birthday I ignored him. Well, talk of giving a dog a bad name, Juana Musante got it into her head that I was taking advantage of the cover of darkness to slip out before supper and wander halfway down the block just to get a glimpse of the cute little number who works at the tire shop. It's like I said. Musante sees everything through a cloud of jealousy. She knows I'm always here, ready to step into the breach so to speak, yet she went and told Zarlenga that I'd managed to nip into the laundry with sinful intentions. The man came at me like boiling milk, and he was right. If it hadn't been for Mr. Renovales, who with his own hand put a piece of raw meat on my eye, I might have lost my temper. There's nothing in all those stories of hers, though I must admit that Juana Musante has a knockout figure. But a guy like me who's had one affair with a girl who is now a manicurist and another with a sixteen-year-old who was going to be a radio star, isn't going to be bowled over by a bundle of curves that may attract attention in Banderaló but that leaves us city boys cold.

"As 'Goggles' says in his little column in the *Evening Chronicle,* the very arrival of Tadeo Limardo at the New Impartial is steeped in mystery. He appeared during carnival in a hail of pistols and stink bombs, but he won't see another carnival. They dressed him in a wooden overcoat and he took up residence in the graveyard. Where are the snows of yesteryear?

"With the beat of the town throbbing in my veins, I had swiped a bear costume from the kitchen boy, a misanthrope who doesn't take to the milonga and doesn't go to dances. Dressed in that costume, I figured I wouldn't be spotted, and I amused myself taking a bow in the back patio before I walked out like a gentleman going for a stroll. As you know, that night the mercury hit a record high. It was so hot that people couldn't help laughing. By evening there were nine sunstroke cases and other casualties of the heat wave. Just picture it, me with my hairy muzzle, sweating blood, but tempted every now and again to take off my bear's head down in some murky alley that if City Hall saw they'd hang their heads in shame. But I tell you, when I have a brainstorm I'm a fanatic. I swear I didn't take that headpiece off just in case one of the boys from the market was around that neck of the woods, the Plaza del Once. By now my lungs were beginning to enjoy the air in the plaza that reeked of barbecue stands and roasting meat. Then I passed out right in front of an old man who was dressed up like Coco the Clown. For the last thirty-eight years he hasn't let a single carnival go by without dousing the policeman who's his neighbor out in Temperley. This old veteran, in spite of his white hairs, had ice water in his veins. With one fell swoop he removed my bear's head but not my ears, because they were glued on. I think either he or his father, who was decked out in a bonnet, pinched my bear head, but I'm not holding it against them. They made me gulp down a thick soup that they forced into my mouth with a wooden spoon. It was so hot that I came to. The trouble is that now the kitchen boy is no longer talking to me, because he suspects the bear's head I lost is the same one that Dr. Rodolfo Carbone was photographed in on one of the floats. Speaking of floats, one of them, driven by some joker with a pack of angels on the back, agreed to drop me off at home, seeing that carnivals have a way of straggling on and on and I couldn't drag my feet another inch. My new friends threw me onto the back of the truck, and I quit the place with a chuckle of relief. I was riding the float like a prince, and I had to laugh. Skirting the wall by the railway tracks came this yokel on foot, a half-starved corpse with a pasty face, who was shuffling along with a little cardboard suitcase and half-open paper bag. One of the angels managed to butt in where it was none of his business and told the hayseed to climb aboard. Just to keep the game going, I shouted to the driver that this was no garbage truck. One of the girls laughed at my joke, and on the spot I made a date to meet her at the empty lot on Humahuaco Street, but I never made it because it was so close to the Wholesale Market. I said I lived around the Haymarket, so they wouldn't think I was down-and-out. But Renovales, who has no finesse, bellowed at me from the sidewalk, because Big Jackoff had lost fifteen cents from his vest while he was in the toilet, and everyone accused me of spending it on ice cream. To make things worse, less than half a block away my clinical eye spotted the cadaver with the suitcase. He was stumbling along exhausted. Cutting short my goodbyes, which are always painful, I jumped off the float as best I could and slipped into the hotel doorway so as to avoid a *casus belli* with the exhausted man. But it's what I always say. Try reasoning with a half-starved man. I was leaving the sixty-cent rooms, where I had just exchanged the bear costume that was roasting me alive for a vegetable salad and emulsion of homemade wine, when out in the front patio I ran straight into the yokel, who didn't even return my greeting.

"What a coincidence. The cadaver spent exactly eleven days in the old drawing room, which, of course, opens onto the first patio. As you know, the people who sleep there are proud as peacocks. Take Big Jackoff, for instance, who panhandles just for the fun of it, although some say he's a millionaire. At first, there were plenty of know-it-alls who predicted that the yokel would soon be exposed, because he was out of his element. Their suspicions were proved wrong. I'll bet you can't name a single person in that room who made any complaints. Nobody spread any rumors or made a fuss. The newcomer behaved perfectly. He ate his stew on time, never pawned a single blanket, never shortchanged anyone, never littered the premises with horsehair looking for the money that some romantics think will tumble out of mattresses. I openly offered him my services for any errands within the hotel itself. I remember that one foggy day I even fetched him a pack of Nobleza cigarettes from the barbershop, and he gave me one to put behind my ear. I never think of that without tipping my hat to him.

"One Saturday, when he had almost recovered, he told us that fifty cents was all he had left. I chuckled to myself at the thought that Sunday, first thing, Zarlenga would confiscate his suitcase and then throw him into the street without a stitch on for not being able to pay for his bed. Like everything human, the New Impartial has its flaws, but from the point of view of discipline the hotel is more like a jail than anything else. Before dawn, I tried to wake up the three good-time Charlies who live in the attic room and spend the whole day making fun of the Great Profile and talking about soccer. Believe it or not, these good-for-nothings missed the performance, but they can't blame me for that. The night before, I tipped them off by circulating a note saying 'Flash! Who are they going to toss out? The answer: Tune in tomorrow.' But I have to admit that they didn't miss much. Claudio Zarlenga let us down. His mind works like a bingo game, and nobody knows what he'll come up with next. Until a little after nine in the morning I stuck to my guns, arguing with the cook about having skipped the soup course and making myself look suspicious to Juana Musante, who claimed that I'd been on the roof trying to make off with the laundry. If I try to add all this up, it comes to nothing. At about seven on the dot, fully dressed, the yokel came out into the patio, where Zarlenga was sweeping. Do you think he stopped to consider that the other man held a broom in his hand? No, sir. He spoke like an open book. I didn't hear what they were saying, but Zarlenga gave him a pat on the shoulder, and for me the show was over.

"I held my head and couldn't believe it. I spent two more hours sweltering on the roof, in hopes of further developments, until the heat got the better of me. When I came down, the yokel was busy in the kitchen, and he didn't hesitate to offer me a nice little bowl of soup. Being an open-minded man, I'll talk to anyone. I started to chat, and after picking apart the topics of the day I found out where he came from. He came from Banderaló, and I figured he was a private eye sent by Juana Musante's husband to spy on her. In order to clear up the doubt that nagged me, I told him of a case which is bound to thrill the listener. It's the story of a shoe coupon—exchangeable for a fishnet undershirt—which Fineberg passed on to the draper's niece, pretending he hadn't noticed that it was already redeemed. You'll never believe it if I tell you that the hayseed wasn't at all moved by my vivid account. And he didn't keel over when I revealed that when Fineberg turned in the coupon he was actually wearing the undershirt. His victim completely missed the significance of the garment he was wearing, as she was hypnotized by his sweet talk and off-color stories. I found out that our yokel was engaged in a business that had him bound hand and foot. Point-blank, I asked what his name was. His back to the wall, my friend had no time to invent a lie, and told me his name was Tadeo Limardo, a fact I was equally quick to accept, since it was a piece of new merchandise, *si você m'entende*. If you're a cop, I'll be a cop and a half, I said to myself, and I followed him everywhere on the sly until I'd worn him out. That same afternoon he promised that if I kept following him like a dog he'd give me a taste of molar stew. My suspicions turned out to be fully justified—the man had something to hide. Just imagine my position. I was on the heels of the mystery and at the same time had to remain confined in my cell of a room, just as if the cook was on one of his rampages.

"I assure you that the scene in the hotel that afternoon was pretty dull. The female element had suffered a great depletion, because Juana Musante had gone to Gorchs until the next day.

"On Monday I showed my face as if nothing had happened, and made a personal appearance in the dining room. The cook, true to his principles, passed by me with his pail of soup and didn't serve me. I then realized that this tyrant was going to condemn me to a starvation siege because I'd played truant the evening before. So I lied to him and said I wasn't hungry.

The man, who's a living contradiction, served me two huge helpings that will stick with me to the grave and left me feeling solid as a tree trunk.

"While the others were laughing their heads off, the yokel, with his mournful face that spoiled the party, shoved aside the bowl of soup with his elbow. On my father's grave, Mr. Parodi, I swear I longed for the moment the cook would slam home a reminder that his soup lay untouched, but Limardo intimidated him with a stony look, and the cook had to pack up his fiddle. Me, I had to laugh. At that moment, Juana Musante came in, eyes flashing with fury and waggling those hips of hers that make me feel I need oxygen. She's always after me, that filly, but I play the unknown soldier. With that crazy way she has of not looking at me, she started collecting the bowls and told the cook, alias the Enemy of Man, that if he wanted to fight with skunks like me he'd better do it and leave her to get on with the work. Suddenly she came face to face with Limardo, and was taken aback to see he hadn't touched his soup. Limardo looked at her as if he had never seen a woman before. There was no doubt about it. The sleuth was struggling to fix in his eye that unforgettable face. The scene, so appealing in its human simplicity, fell apart when Juana told the gawker that since he'd obviously been sleeping alone for some time why didn't he go back to the country for a breath of fresh air. Busy as he was making pellets of bread—an ugly habit the cook has cured me of— Limardo failed to respond to her considerate advice.

"A few hours later, a scene took place which if I describe will make you thank the law for keeping you locked up. At seven in the evening, following an old habit of mine, I had popped out into the first patio intending to intercept the stewed tripe that the tycoons in the old drawing room order from the corner shop. With all your brains, I'll bet you still can't guess who I saw. Pardo Salivazo in person, wearing a narrow-brimmed hat, a tight-fitting suit, and Fray Mocho shoes. Seeing this old friend of mine from the Wholesale Market was all I needed to make me lock myself in my room for a solid week. Three days later, Fineberg told me I could come out, since Pardo had vanished without paying. He'd also taken all the third patio's light bulbs, except the one Fineberg had in his pocket. I figured Fineberg, with his mania for airing the room, had dreamed up this story just to get rid of me, but I stayed put as if I owned the place until the end of the week, when the cook drove me out. I must admit that this time the Profile had spoken the truth. My pleasure in discovering this was interrupted by a trivial—even negligible—event that only a man with a sharp eye could have spotted. Limardo had moved from the old drawing room into one of the sixty-cent bunks. As he couldn't come up with the cash, they made him work for his keep. To me, a light sleeper, the whole affair smelled like a sleuth's scheme to worm his way into the running of the establishment so he could collect information about the staff's movements. He helped with the bookkeeping, and with this as an excuse the yokel spent the whole day poking around the office. I personally have no regular job in the place even if I sometimes give the cook a hand so as not to look too selfish. Anyway, I ambled up and down in front of his desk to emphasize the difference between us, until Mr. Renovales made a fatherly remark that sent me scurrying back to my room.

"Twenty days later, a well-founded rumor had it that Mr. Renovales wanted to throw Limardo out and that Zarlenga was against it. I wouldn't swallow this, even if I saw it in black and white. If you don't mind, I'll give you the facts the way I see them. Can you really picture Mr. Renovales punishing such a poor devil? Can you imagine Zarlenga, with his morals, siding with justice even for a moment? Forget it, my dear friend; don't delude yourself. The truth turned out to be the other way around. Zarlenga was always getting after Limardo. He was the one who wanted to throw the yokel out. It was Renovales who stood up for him. Let me leak it to you—this personal opinion of mine is backed up by the boys in the attic.

"In fact, it wasn't long before Limardo was moving beyond the narrow limits of the office. He soon spread all over the hotel like spilled oil. One day he was mending the eternal leak in the ceiling of the sixty-cent rooms; the next, he was modernizing the banisters with a stippled paint job; then he cleaned a stain off Zarlenga's trousers; and then they gave him the privilege of washing down the first patio every day, and of polishing the old drawing room like a mirror and clearing it of garbage.

"Because he stuck his nose in where it didn't belong, Limardo kept stirring up trouble. Take, for example, the day the attic gang were having fun painting the hardware-store lady's tabby cat red. I had no part in it. Probably because they guessed I was busy leafing through my Superman comics, which Dr. Escudero had passed on to me. To someone in the know, the case is quite clear. The hardware lady, who's easily upset, was about to accuse one of the gang of stealing a funnel and some corks. The boys resented it and decided to take it out on the person of the cat. Limardo became the fly in the ointment. He took the half-painted cat away from them and at the risk of a fractured skull and the intervention of the SPCA, threw the animal into the back of the hardware store. Mr. Parodi, don't remind me what they did to the yokel. The boys jumped him. They laid him on the floor, one sat on his stomach, another stepped on his face, the third made him gargle paint. I would gladly have contributed an additional wallop, but I swear I was scared the yokel might recognize me in spite of being dazed from the thrashing he got. Besides, you have to admit that the gang are very touchy, and if I butted in I might have got walloped myself. Then Renovales appeared, and everyone took off. Two of them managed to reach the pantry. Another tried to imitate my example and vanish into the chicken coop, but Renovales' heavy hand gave him a warning. When I saw this fatherly reaction I wanted to applaud, but on second thought I only chuckled. The yokel picked himself up. He looked like hell, but he got what he deserved. With his own hand, Mr. Zarlenga brought him an eggnog and made him drink it right down, saying encouragingly, 'Come on, now. Take it like a man.'

"Please, Mr. Parodi, don't get the wrong idea about life in the hotel from the incident with the cat. We have our good times too, and if there are fights that are bitter at the time, later I can look back on them philosophically and laugh at the fun I've had. For example, let me tell you the story of the blue-penciled circular. There are cops who don't miss a trick, but despite their brains and cunning they can bore you to death. Yet for picking up fresh news, juicy news, nobody holds a candle to me. One Tuesday, I cut out a few paper hearts, because a little bird told me that Josephine Mamberto, the draper's niece, was going out with Fineberg in order to get back the coupon undershirt. To let even the Impartial's flies in on the news,

I wrote on each heart a witty note—of course, in a disguised hand—which said, 'Flash! Who's marrying J.M. every second day? Answer: A boarder in an undershirt.' I personally saw to the distribution of this joke. When nobody was looking, I slipped it under all the doors, even the toilets. I'm telling you, that day I had about as much appetite for food as for kissing my own elbow. But I was itching to see how the joke had gone down, and, feeling obliged to confront the usual Tuesday meal of leftovers, I went to the dining room early. There I sat on my bit of the bench, large as life, in my undershirt, banging my spoon on the table to hurry things up. Just then the cook appeared, and I pretended to be absorbed in reading one of the hearts. You should have seen him move! Before I could get under the table he'd lifted me up with his right hand and with his left squashed my little hearts against my nose, wrinkling them all up. Don't blame him for being burned up, Mr. Parodi. It was my fault. After having distributed that joke, there I was in an undershirt, making matters worse.

"On the sixth of May, at some hour or other, a face chewing on a local cigar appeared a few inches from Zarlenga's inkwell, the one with the statue of Napoleon on it. Zarlenga, who can pull the wool over any customer's eyes, was trying to convince an honest beggar of the hotel's respectability. This man was the leading light of the Society for Distressed Gentlefolk, and even the Unzué Asylum would have been proud to have him at one of their open days. In an effort to lure the bearded man into taking room and board, Zarlenga had offered him the gasper. This character in sackcloth, who was nobody's fool, plucked it from the air and lit it at once, just like a pope. No sooner had this selfish Smokaloni taken a trial puff when the contraption exploded, adding a new sooty smudge to his already grubby face. What a sorry sight he was. We all held our sides with laughter. After this hilarity, the man in the sack fled, depriving the cash register of a considerable sum. Zarlenga went into a rage and asked who was the joker who planted the cigar. My motto is never get mixed up with temperamental types. Nipping back to my room, I almost crashed headlong into the yokel, who stood there with his eyes popping out like he was in a trance. He must have been so scared he ran the wrong way, because he dived straight into the wolf's mouth, that is to say into Zarlenga's office. He burst in without knocking, which is always a bad thing, and, facing Zarlenga, said, 'I'm responsible for the joke cigar. I just felt like it.'

"Vanity is Limardo's downfall, I thought to myself. What was the point of doing that? Why didn't he let someone else take the blame? A guy with his head screwed on never gives himself away. If you'd only seen what Zarlenga did. He shrugged his shoulders and spat on the floor just as if he weren't in his own house. His anger suddenly vanished, and he seemed to drift into a daydream. I think he eased up afraid that if he gave Limardo what he deserved a few of us would have slipped out that very night, taking advantage of the deep sleep that follows heavy exercise. Limardo stood there looking like a loaf that nobody wants to buy, and the boss won a moral victory that made us all proud. Ipso facto I smelled a rat. The joke wasn't the yokel's doing, because everybody had seen Fineberg's sister going out with one of the owners of the Joke Shop at the corner of Pueyrredon and Valentín Gómez.

"It pains me to tell you something that I know will touch you to the core, Mr. Parodi, but on the day after the explosion a crisis shattered our peace and worried even those of us who never take anything seriously. It's easy to talk about it, but you really needed to have been there. Zarlenga and Juana Musante had a fight. I can't imagine what could possibly have started such a fracas in the New Impartial. Ever since the time that half-pint Turk, armed with a blunted pair of scissors and whooping like an Indian, did in Tigre Bengolea just before the soup course, any disturbance, any argument, is officially prohibited by the management. That's why nobody hesitates to give the cook a hand when he's pounding reason into a hooligan. But the example must come from above. If the top brass engage in lawlessness, what will become of the rest of us, the mass of boardinghouse lodgers? I can tell you that I've lived through bitter moments, with my spirits sagging, without moral guidance. You can say what you like about me, but when the chips are down you can't say I'm defeatist. Why sow panic? My lips were sealed. Every few minutes, on some pretext or other, I marched up and down the corridor that led to the office where Zarlenga and Musante were going at it hot and heavy without once indulging in good old straightforward insult. And then I'd rush up to the garret, announcing with a superior air, 'Gossip! Gossip!' Deep in their game of rummy, these elitists paid no attention to me. But a persistent dog gets his bone. Limardo, who was picking the dirt out of Big Jackoff's comb with his fingernail, was forced to listen. Before I could finish, he got up as if it was coffee break and disappeared in the direction of the office. I crossed myself and tailed him like a shadow. Suddenly he turned around and spoke in a voice that demanded obedience. 'Make yourself useful and round up all the lodgers at once.' He didn't have to tell me twice. I collected the whole filthy bunch. To a man, we gathered around, except for the Great Profile, who scampered off, and later we found out that the toilet chain was missing. That living gallery made up a cross-section of society. Rubbing shoulders were the introvert and the joker, the ninety-five center and the sixty, the con man and Big Jackoff, the beggar and the panhandler, the nameless pickpocket without portfolio and the renowned burglar. Once again the hotel seemed to be its old self. It was more a frieze than a picture—the people following their shepherd; all of us, in a state of utter confusion, convinced that Limardo was our leader. When he reached the office, he opened the door without bothering to knock. I whispered to myself, 'Savastano, back to your room.' The voice of reason rang out in the wilderness, but I was surrounded by a wall of enthusiasts, who prevented my retreat.

"Though half blinded by nerves, I could still make out a scene that even a tango singer like Lorusso couldn't have made clearer. Zarlenga was half hidden behind Limardo, but I could ogle the buxom Juana Musante as much as I liked. She was wearing her red bathrobe and bunny-fur slippers with pompoms, and I had to prop myself up against one of the ninety-five centers. Limardo, ready to burst, held the center of the stage. We all more or less understood that the Impartial was about to have a change of bosses. We could already feel our spines tingling at the blows that Limardo was going to deal Zarlenga.

"Instead, Limardo fell back on words, which are no use at all in solving a mystery. He spoke with his golden tongue, saying things that are still fermenting in my brain. At times like this, the speaker usually turns out to be a solemn quibbler, but Limardo, dispensing with all formality, fired a direct salvo in plain language about disagreement and discord. He said that marriage was a unity, and one had to be terribly careful not to split it up. He insisted that Juana Musante and Zarlenga should kiss in front of everyone so that the clientele would know they loved each other.

"You should have seen Zarlenga! Faced with such sensible advice, he stood there like a zombie and didn't know what to do. But Musante, who has her head screwed on, isn't the type to swallow such bouquets. She shot up as if he had criticized her cooking. The sight of her towering rage was enough to make me a candidate for the loony bin. Juana Musante did not mince matters. She lashed into the yokel and said he should look after his own marriage if he had one, and if he poked his snout in her affairs again they'd chop it off. To put an end to the argument, Zarlenga admitted that Mr. Renovales—who at the time was around the corner having a beer—had been right in wanting to throw Limardo out. Zarlenga ordered him to leave on the spot, without considering that it was already after eight. Limardo, the poor fool, had to pack his suitcase and paper bag in a hurry, but his hands were so shaky that Simon Fineberg offered to help him. In the turmoil, the yokel lost a bone-handled jackknife and a flannel undershirt. The yokel's eyes filled with tears as he looked around for the last time at the place that had given him a roof. He nodded goodbye and disappeared into the night, destination unknown.

"Early the next morning, Limardo woke me, bringing a cup of maté that I greedily sipped without asking any questions about how he'd come back. That maté still burns my tongue. You may say that Limardo was behaving like an anarchist when he disobeyed the landlord. But it's tough being deprived of a place that's become second nature to you after you've been through so much to get it.

"My hasty guzzling of the maté made me feel guilty, so I decided to stay in my room, playing sick. A few days later, when I ventured out again, one of the jokers informed me that Zarlenga had tried again to chuck Limardo out, but the yokel threw himself to the floor and let himself be kicked and beaten, overpowering Zarlenga by passive resistance. Fineberg never confirmed any of this. He selfishly hogs everything so as to keep me in the dark about even basic items of gossip. But from personal experience I know that Limardo was given a folding bed and a small can of kerosene in the broom closet under the stairs. The advantage was that he was able to hear everything that went on in Zarlenga's room, because there was only a thin partition between them. I was the victim of this new move. The brooms, after having been counted and inventoried, were moved into my room thanks to Fineberg's Machiavellian scheming. He had them placed in my half.

"This shows you what Fineberg's like. He's obviously a fanatic when it comes to brooms. As for the peace and quiet of the hotel, first he provokes the jokers and Limardo, then he gets them to bury the hatchet. Since the squabble over the red paint and the cat had long been forgotten, Fineberg had to refresh the memory of the warring parties, goading them on with insults and abuse. When there was nothing left for them but to throw their boots at each other or else kick each other with them on, Fineberg managed to turn their attention to the subject of medicinal wines. I must confess he knows a lot about them, because only a few days before Dr. Pertiné slipped him a prospectus with an order blank for bottles and half-bottles of Apache, 'a great health wine,' so the label says, 'authorized by Dr. Pertiné.' I've always said that alcohol's a great pacifier, although when used to excess it forces the New Impartial's management to take action. The fact is that by telling them that it was three against one and the one carried a gun, Fineberg persuaded them that union was strength and that if they wanted to drink to it he'd provide the refreshment at a ridiculously low price. The pinchpenny impulse we all share came out. They bought twelve bottles and by the time they were bending elbows on the eighth they were already the Drunken Quartet. The jokers, who are selfishness itself, didn't notice that I was hovering around with a little glass of my own, until the yokel pointed out in jest that they ought not to neglect me, because I wasn't the only dog. I took advantage of their peals of laughter to take a gulp, although it wasn't much more than a thimbleful, because you have to get used to wine, which soon comes to taste like honey, and your tongue thickens just as if you'd lapped up a pot of syrup. Fineberg, with his fondness for pawnbrokers, was also interested in firearms. He said they charged Limardo very little for the blunderbuss he carried in his belt, and Fineberg offered to get him another one just like it even cheaper. If their conversation had already become distinctly heated, you can imagine the effect when the Great Profile sent up this balloon. There were more opinions than you could shake a stick at. According to Big Jackoff, buying a new gun was a quick way of getting your name in the police records. A couple of the jokers argued about different shooting ranges. I put in the one about all guns being loaded by the devil. Limardo, who was completely sozzled, said he'd come with a revolver because he was planning to kill someone. Fineberg told the story of a Jew who didn't want to buy a gun from him, and the next night he and his friends gave the man a scare with a chocolate pistol.

"The following day, to show my interest, I sidled up to the hotel staff, who often met out in the patio to sip a few matés and talk over the day's plan of action. Even the smartest lodger can learn something there, though you may have to put up with hearing a few home truths. And of course you run the risk of being caught eavesdropping. If that happens you're taken apart like a Meccano toy. Anyway, there they were, the Holy Trinity, as the three jokers call them—Zarlenga, Musante, and Renovales. The fact that they didn't shoo me off encouraged me a bit. I ambled in nonchalantly and to make sure they wouldn't throw me right out I promised them a plum of gossip. I told them all about the reconciliation, and I didn't leave out the business of Limardo's revolver or Fineberg's medicinal wine either. You should have seen the sour faces. To be on the safe side I skedaddled before any gossipmonger could say I was telling tales to the management—a thing I'd never do.

"I beat a careful retreat, but kept a beady eye on the trio's movements. Pretty soon Zarlenga strode off to the broom closet where the yokel slept. Agile as a monkey, I scrambled up the stairs and put my ear to the step so as not to lose a word of what was being said below. Zarlenga demanded that the yokel turn in the revolver. Limardo flatly refused. Zarlenga threatened to do something to him which I'd rather spare you from hearing, Mr. Parodi. With a sort of calm pride, Limardo said that threats couldn't hurt him, because he was as invulnerable as if he were wearing a bullet-proof vest, and it would take more than one Zarlenga to scare him. *Inter nos,* the vest wasn't much use to him, if he had one, because it wasn't too long before he was found dead in my room."

"How did the argument end?" asked Parodi.

"The way everything ends. Zarlenga wasn't going to waste time on a poor lunatic. He left as he came—inconspicuously.

"Now we arrive at the fatal Sunday. I'm sorry to say that's always a dead day at the hotel. As I was bored stiff, I decided to pluck Fineberg from his abysmal ignorance and teach him to play *truco,* so as to save him from making a fool of himself in every corner bar. Mr. Parodi, as a teacher I'm a natural. The ipso facto proof is that my pupil won two pesos off me, of which he collected one peso forty in change, and to square the debt he asked me to invite him to a matinee at the Excelsior. They're right when they say that Rosie Rosenberg is the queen of comedy. The audience laughed as if they were being tickled to death, but I couldn't make out a word, because they were talking in some sort of Jewish lingo that nobody can understand, not even another Jew, and I was dying to get back to the hotel so that Fineberg could explain the jokes. But it was no joke when I reached my room. What a sight my bed was! Both the spread and the blanket were one big stain and the pillow was no better. The blood had soaked right through to the mattress, and I wondered where I was going to sleep that night, because the late Tadeo Limardo was stretched out on the bed, deader than a salami.

"Naturally my first thought was for the hotel. I didn't want anyone thinking it was me who'd carved Limardo up and stained all the bedclothes. It was obvious that the corpse was not going to amuse Zarlenga at all. And it didn't, because the cops questioned him until way past eleven, which is long after lights-out at the New Impartial. While I was thinking this over, I was screaming at the top of my voice, because I'm like Napoleon when it comes to doing two things at once. I'm not exaggerating. The whole place came running, including the kitchen boy, who stuffed a rag in my mouth and almost had another corpse on his hands. Fineberg was there, and so was Juana Musante, the jokers, the cook, Big Jackoff, and finally Mr. Renovales. We all spent the next day at the police station. I was in my element, answering everything they threw at me and giving such a fantastic performance that they were all thunderstruck. I didn't forget a single clue. I produced Exhibit A, the fact that Limardo had been snuffed out with his own bone-handled jackknife at around five o'clock in the afternoon.

"Look, all these people who think this case is a mystery don't know what they're talking about, because it would have been far more mysterious if the crime had taken place at night, when the hotel's full of strangers that I would hardly call residents, since they only pay for the use of a bed and an hour later disappear.

"Except for Fineberg and me, almost everyone was in the hotel when the murder took place. We only found out later that at the crucial moment Zarlenga wasn't there. He'd been out in Saavedra, at a cockfight, where he was fighting Father Argañaraz's white cock."

II

A week later, an excited and happy Tulio Savastano burst into the cell. "I've done your little errand, sir," he babbled out. "Here's my boss!"

Savastano was followed by an asthmatic man, clean-shaven, with blue eyes and a thick mop of gray hair. His clothes were neat and dark. He wore a vicuña shawl, and Parodi noticed that his fingernails were polished. The two gentlemen sat at their ease on the pair of stools. Almost falling all over himself with servility, Savastano paced up and down and up and down the small cell.

"Room Number 42, this fellow here, gave me your message," said the gray-haired man. "Look, if it's to talk about this Limardo business it has nothing to do with me. I'm sick of the whole thing. At the hotel nobody talks about anything else. If you know anything about it, sir, you'd better get in touch with young Pagola, who's in charge of the case. I'm sure he'll be very grateful, because the police are running around in circles like chickens with their heads off."

"Who do you take me for, don Zarlenga?" said Parodi. "I steer clear of that Mafia. Of course, I have a few insights, which, if you'll do me the honor of listening to, you may not regret.

"If you don't mind, let's start with Limardo. This young man here, Savastano, who's as bright as they come, took him for a spy sent by Señora Juana Musante's husband. With all due respect, why drag a spy into the story?* Limardo was an employee of the Banderaló post office. In fact, he was the lady's husband. You're not going to deny this, are you?

"Look, I'm going to tell you the whole story as I see it. You ran off with Limardo's wife and left him eating his heart out back in Banderaló. Three years later, the

*Entia non sunt multiplicanda praeter necessitate—Entities are not to be multiplied without necessity. [Footnote submitted by Dr. William Ockham.]

man couldn't stand it any longer and decided to come to Buenos Aires. Somehow or other he made the journey; all we know is that he arrived in a state of exhaustion during carnival. He'd put all his money and health into hock to make a desperate pilgrimage, and, what's worse, all he got for his trouble was to be shut away for ten days before he could see the woman for whom he had beggared himself so far away. Those ten days at ninety cents each used up all his money.

"Partly out of bravado, partly out of pity, you spread it around that Limardo was quite a man. You even went as far as making him out to be a tough guy. Later, when you saw him come into your hotel, without a peso to his name, you went out of your way to be kind to him, adding insult to injury. This is where the counterpoint began. You were busy humiliating him; he, humiliating himself. You relegated him to a sixty-cent room in the garret, and on top of that made him look after the books. Nothing was too much for him, so after a few days he was mending the roof and even cleaning your trousers. The first time she clapped eyes on him, his wife told him to get out.

"Renovales agreed, fed up with the man's behavior and with your treatment of him. Limardo stayed on in the hotel and sought new humiliations. One day, a few jobless wonders were painting a cat. Limardo interfered, not out of compassion but because he was looking for a beating. They beat him up all right, and on top of it you made him swallow an eggnog and more than one insult. Then we come to the cigar. The Jew's joke cost your hotel the custom of a genuine beggar. Limardo took the blame, but this time you didn't punish him, because you were beginning to suspect that he might be up to something very ugly with all his self-humiliation. But up until then it had only been a matter of blows and insults. Limardo was out for something closer to home. When you and your wife were fighting, the man collected an audience and asked you to make up and kiss in front of everyone. Just imagine what that meant—a husband gathering onlookers to ask his wife and her paramour to love each other again. You threw him out. The next day he was back, serving maté to the most pathetic creep in the hotel. Then came passive resistance, which is just a way of getting yourself kicked. To wear him down, you allotted him that mousehole next to your room, where he could hear every word you two whispered to each other.

"Later on, Limardo let the Jew make peace between him and the jokers. He went along with this, since his plan was to be humiliated by everyone. He even insulted himself, placing himself on the same level as this gent here. He called himself a dog. That evening drink loosened his tongue, and he said he'd brought a revolver with him to kill someone. A certain gossip-monger relayed this tale to the hotel management. You wanted to throw Limardo out again, but he stood up to you and told you he was invulnerable. You didn't quite understand what he was talking about, but you got scared. Now we come to the tricky bit."

Savastano squatted down to hear better. Parodi looked at him distractedly and asked him politely to leave, for perhaps it might be unwise for him to hear the rest. Dumbfounded, Savastano could hardly get to the door fast enough.

Parodi went on unhurriedly. "A few days earlier, this young man who's just favored us with his absence, had discovered some sort of involvement between Fineberg and a Miss Josephine Mamberto of the drapery shop. He wrote a bit of nonsense on some little paper hearts, and instead of names he used initials.

Your lady wife, who saw those hearts, took J.M. to be Juana Musante. She made your cook beat Savastano up, and on top of that she held a grudge against him. She too had suspected there was something behind Limardo's self-humiliation. When she learned he had a revolver and intended to kill someone, she knew she wasn't threatened. Her fear was for you. She knew Limardo was a coward. She figured he was piling ignominy upon ignominy so as to put himself in an impossible situation where he would have to kill. The lady was right. The man was determined to kill. But not you —somebody else.

"Sunday was a dead day in the hotel, as your companion said. You had gone out. You were in Saavedra with Father Argañaraz's fighting cock. Limardo made his way into your room with the revolver in his hand. Mrs. Musante, who saw him, thought he'd come to kill you. She loathed him so much that she had no qualms about stealing his knife when he was thrown out. Now she used that knife to kill him. Limardo, even with the gun in his hand, offered no resistance. Juana Musante put the body on Savastano's cot to get back at him for the tale of the hearts. As you may remember, Savastano and Fineberg were at the movies.

"In the end, Limardo got what he wanted. It was true that he had brought a gun to kill someone, but that someone was himself. He had come a long way. For months and months, he had begged for abuse and insult in order to strengthen his nerve to kill himself, because death was what he longed for. I also think that before he died he wanted to see his wife."

Pujato,
September 2, 1942

Tai An's Long Search

To the memory of Ernest Bramah

I

That's all I needed, thought Isidro Parodi, almost out loud. A four-eyed Japanese!

Without relinquishing his straw hat and umbrella, Dr. Shu T'ung, accustomed to the ways of the great embassies, kissed the hand of the inmate of cell 273.

"Will you permit the body of a foreigner to abuse this honorable stool?" he asked with a voice like a bird in perfect Spanish. "The quadruped is wooden and has no objection. My humble name is Shu T'ung and, in the face of universal opprobrium, I hold the office of cultural attaché at the Chinese Embassy, an unworthy and unwholesome hovel. My shapeless narrative has already grated each of Dr. Montenegro's most wise ears. This phoenix of criminal investigation is as unfailing as the tortoise, but he is also as majestic and ponderous as an astronomical observatory wondrously buried by the sands of the barren desert. It is true to say that in order to catch a grain of rice nine fingers on each hand are not a superfluous endowment. I, who by the tacit agreement of barbers and hatters have but one head, aspire to crown myself with two heads renowned for their shrewdness—Dr. Montenegro's, which is considerable, and yours, which is the size of a porpoise. With all his palaces and libraries, even the Yellow Emperor was forced to admit that a bream plucked from the ocean is unlikely to enjoy old age and the veneration of its grandchildren. Far from being an old bream, I am scarcely a young man. What am I to do now that the abyss is opening like a succulent oyster to devour me? And yet this is not merely about my wretched self. The extraordinary Madame Hsin, owing to the pillars of the law—whose tireless vigilance causes her despair and inconvenience—has been dosing herself with veronal night after night. The police seem not to have taken into consideration that her protector has been murdered in very disquieting circumstances, and that she, now a helpless orphan, has been left in charge of the Bewildered Dragon, a flourishing dance hall located near the waterfront, at the corner of Leandro Alem and Tucumán Street. Ah, the stoical and many-faceted Madame Hsin! While her right eye weeps for the loss of a friend, her left eye must laugh to excite the sailors.

"Ah, your poor ears! To expect eloquence and information from my mouth is to expect the caterpillar to speak with the composure of the dromedary or even with the range of crickets in a cage wrought of cardboard and painted in the twelve prescribed colors. I am not the extraordinary Meng-tse who, in foretelling the appearance of the new moon before the College of Astronomy, spoke for twenty-nine years at a stretch, until his children were obliged to take over. It cannot be denied that I don't have the same amount of time at my disposal, nor am I a Meng-tse, nor is the number of your many and praiseworthy ears greater than that of the busy ants who tunnel the earth. I am no orator.

My speech will be as short as if delivered by a dwarf. I have no five-stringed instrument. My speech will be both inaccurate and tedious.

"You may submit me to the most refined instruments of torture hoarded in this many-faceted palace should I again reveal to your well-stocked memory the secret rites of the cult of the Demon of the Terrible Awakening. This, as you were just about to say, is a magical deistic sect, which recruits disciples from the guild of beggars and actors and which only a sinologist like you, a European surrounded by the tinkle of teacups, knows like your own back.

"Nineteen years ago there took place the dastardly deed which weakened the legs of the world and echoes of which reached this horrified city. My tongue, which is clumsier than a brick, has remembered the theft of the goddess's talisman. In the middle of Yunnan is a secret lake; in the middle of this lake, an island; in the middle of the island, a sanctuary. In the sanctuary the statue of the goddess stands in its splendor; in the statue's halo glows the talisman. To describe this jewel in a rectangular room is unwise. I shall say only that it is of jade, that it casts no shadow, that its exact size is that of a walnut, and that its essential powers are wisdom and magic. Minds perverted by the missionaries pretend to deny the existence of these powers, but should any mortal seize the talisman and hold it outside the temple for twenty years he will become the secret king of the world. Yet this is idle speculation. From the earliest dawn of time until the last sunset, the jewel will remain in the sanctuary, even if for the past eighteen years—the fleeting present—a thief has kept it hidden.

"The head priest entrusted the magician Tai An with the restoration of the jewel. As everyone knows, he sought a favorable conjunction of the planets, undertook the necessary procedures, and put his ear to the ground. He heard distinctly the footsteps of every man on earth, and at once recognized those of the thief. These distant footsteps wandered the length and breadth of a remote city—a city of mud and paradise trees, without wooden pillows or porcelain towers, surrounded by wastes of grass and dark water. The city was hidden in the West beyond many sunsets. In order to reach it, Tai An faced the risks of a steamship propelled by smoke. He disembarked in Semarang after twenty-three days in the bowels of a Danish ship with a herd of pigs and no food or drink other than an inexhaustible succession of Dutch cheeses. In Capetown, he joined the honorable guild of garbage collectors, and he played his part in the Fetid Week strike. A year later, an ignorant mob clamored in the streets and alleyways of Montevideo for the meager cornstarch wafers sold by a young man dressed like a foreigner. This nutritive young man was Tai An. After a bloody struggle with the indifference of these carnivores, the magician moved to Buenos Aires, which he guessed would be more receptive to the doctrine of the wafers and where he quickly set up a thriving charcoal business. This sooty establishment brought him to poverty's long, empty table. Weary of these feasts of hunger, Tai An said to himself, 'For the demanding palate, an edible dog; for a man, the Celestial Empire.' And he rushed into business with Samuel Nemirovsky, a highly regarded cabinetmaker who, at the very center of the Once Square, fashions all the wardrobes and screens which his admiring customers 'receive direct from Peking.' The humble shop prospered. Tai An moved from a coalshed to a furnished apartment, located exactly at 347 Deán Funes Street. The steady production of screens and wardrobes did not distract him from his main aim—the recovery of the jewel. He knew for sure that the thief was in Buenos Aires, the remote city that the magical circles and triangles had revealed to him from the island of the temple.

"The athlete of literacy leafs through newspapers in order to keep fit. Less far-ranging and felicitous, Tai An restricted himself to the shipping columns, fearing that the thief might escape or that a ship might bring an accomplice to whom the talisman would be passed on. Tai An was getting as close to the thief as the rings around a stone when it is first thrown into water. Several times he changed his name and quarters. Magic, like the other exact sciences, is little more than the firefly that guides our vain stumbling in the vast night. Tai An's calculations marked the general area where the thief was hiding, but gave no clue as to his house or his identity. Nonetheless, the magician persisted in his tireless aim."

"Neither does the veteran of the Salon Doré tire, and he too persists," Gervasio Montenegro exclaimed with an air of spontaneity. He had been spying on all fours, an eye at the keyhole and his whalebone cane between his teeth. Now, he erupted into the cell wearing a spotless white suit and a straw boater. *De la mesure avant toute chose.* I'm not exaggerating. I have not yet discovered the murderer's address, but I have found the address of this timid client. Cheer him up, my dear Parodi, cheer him up. With all the authority that I am the first to grant you, tell him how this self-made detective called Gervasio Montenegro saved a princess's jewel on an express train and later offered her his hand. But let us direct our powerful spotlights on the all-devouring future. *Messieurs, faites vos jeux.* I'll lay two to one that our diplomatic friend is not here just for the pleasure—praiseworthy, of course—of paying his respects. My now proverbial intuition whispers to me that Dr. T'ung's presence is not unconnected with the strange murder on Deán Funes Street. Ha, ha, ha! I've hit the bull's-eye. But I must not rest on my laurels. Here comes my second salvo; I already see the success of my first one. I'll wager that the doctor has spiced up his story with Oriental mystery, which is the hallmark both of his interesting monosyllables and his color and appearance. Far be it from me to censure him with biblical language, full of sermons and parables. I suspect, however, that you would rather listen to my *compte rendu*—all nerve, muscle, and bone—than to my client's ponderous metaphors."

Once again Dr. Shu T'ung spoke up in his humble way. "Your voluble colleague speaks with the eloquence of an orator who displays a double row of golden teeth. Let me pick up the evil thread of my story and state modestly that just as the sun sees everything while its own brilliance is invisible, Tai An, loyal and tenacious, persisted in his implacable search. He studied the comings and goings of everyone in the Chinese community, while remaining almost unknown to them all. Woe unto the weakness of man! Not even the tortoise is perfect, meditating under its shell dome. The magician's secrecy had one flaw. On a winter's night in 1927, under the arcades of the Once Square, he saw a circle of tramps and beggars laughing at a poor wretch who was lying on the stone pavement, suffering hunger and cold. Tai An's pity was doubled when he found that the object of their contempt was Chinese. The golden man can lend even a tea leaf without losing face. Tai An took home the stranger, whose descriptive name is Fang She, and put him up in Nemirovsky's cabinetmaker's shop.

"I can give neither a very refined nor a pleasant-sounding account of Fang She. If the most lettered of the daily newspapers is not mistaken, he is a native of Yunnan, and he reached this city in 1923—one year before the magician. Several times he received me on Deán Funes Street, always displaying his inherent courtesy. Together we practiced the art of calligraphy in the shade of a weeping willow tree that grows in the patio. Its delicacy reminded him, he once told me, of the thick forests that adorn the banks of the rippling Ling-Kiang."

"Why don't you shut up about calligraphy and adornment," remarked the detective, "and tell me about the people in the house."

"A good actor never comes on stage before the theater is built," replied Shu T'ung. "Firstly, I shall make a feeble attempt to describe the house. Then I shall fail dismally to sketch a portrait of its inhabitants."

"Allow me a word of encouragement," said Montenegro impetuously. "The building on Deán Funes Street is an interesting *masure,* dating from the turn of the century—one of the many examples of our vernacular architecture, in which the naïve contribution of the Italian bricklayer holds its own almost untouched by Le Corbusier's stark Latin principles. I recall it precisely. You can already see the place. On today's façade, yesterday's pale blue has become white and aseptic. Within, the quiet patio of our childhood—where we once saw the black slave girl bustling about with the silver maté cup—endures the tide of progress, which floods it with exotic dragons and thousand-year-old lacquers, offspring of the industrialized Nemirovsky's phony brush! At the rear stands the wooden shed where Fang She lives. Beside it is the green melancholy of the willow tree, which with its leafy hand caresses the exile's homesickness. A heavy wire pig fence, five feet high, separates our property from an empty lot—one of those picturesque *baldíos,* to use the inimitable Argentine word, which still exist unvanquished in the heart of the city and where the alley cat sometimes comes in search of medicinal grasses to ease his pain, the pain of a rooftop *célibataire.* The ground floor is dedicated to the salesroom and the *atelier.* * The upper floor—I mean, *cela va sans dire,* before the fire—served as the hearth and home, the inviolable *chez lui* of Fang She, that particle of the Far East transplanted to the Argentine capital complete with all his native character and failings."

"In the tutor's shoe the pupil puts his foot," said Dr. Shu T'ung. "Following the nightingale's victory, the ears hear and pardon the quacking of the duck. Dr. Montenegro has constructed the house. My thick, unqualified tongue will sketch the people in it. I reserve the highest throne for Madame Hsin."

"It's my lead," said Montenegro just then. "Don't make a mistake that you'll regret, my dear Parodi. Don't dream of confusing Madame Hsin with those *poules de luxe* that you must have endured and adored in the great hotels of the Riviera, where they display their frivolous affluence with an ugly Pekinese and a spotless forty-horsepower motorcar. Madame Hsin is quite another matter. In her we have the formidable

*Not at all. We—contemporaries of the machine gun and biceps—repudiate this delicate rhetoric. I should say, with the finality of a bullet, "I put salesroom and *atelier* on the ground floor. I lock the Chinamen upstairs." [Footnote written in the hand of Carlos Anglada.]

combination of a great society woman and an Oriental tigress. With her slanted eyes, she winks at us, this eternal Venus, this temptress. Her mouth is a single crimson flower. Her hands are silk and ivory. Her figure, set off by a Victorian *cambrure,* is a coquettish vanguard of the yellow peril, and already it has taken over Paquin's canvasses and Schiaparelli's sketches. But a thousand pardons, my dear *confrère.* The poet has outrun the historian in me. To pencil Madame Hsin's portrait I have resorted to pastels. For a likeness of Tai An I shall turn to the virility of the etching. No prejudice, however ingrained, will distort my vision. I shall stick to the photographic documentation of the latest editions of the newspapers. Besides, the race obliterates the individual. We murmur 'Chinaman' and persist in our feverish pursuit of a yellow phantom, perhaps unaware of the banal or grotesque but invincibly human tragedy of this exotic character. Let this same portrait stand for Fang She, whose appearance I still remember perfectly, who has always been receptive to my fatherly advice, whose hands have shaken my kid glove. Now comes a contrast—in the fourth portrait in my gallery we glimpse a distinctly Oriental character. I have neither summoned him nor told him to stay away. He is the foreigner, the Jew, who lurks in the dark background of my story and, so long as wise legislation does not strike him down, will go on lurking at the *carrefours* of history. In this case, our guest is called Samuel Nemirovsky. Let me spare you even the slightest detail concerning this extremely vulgar cabinetmaker: his serene, clear brow; the sad dignity in his eyes; his black prophet's beard; and his height the same as mine."

"Daily commerce in elephants makes even the most discriminating eye insensitive to the ridiculous fly,"

Dr. Shu T'ung suddenly remarked. "I note with squeals of pleasure that my own unworthy portrait does not clutter Mr. Montenegro's gallery. Still, if the voice of a crab means anything, I too have demeaned the house on Deán Funes Street with my presence, although my own imperceptible dwelling place hides from men and gods alike at the corner of Rivadavia and Jujuy. One of my pastimes is the door-to-door sale of mantelpieces, screens, beds, and sideboards, which the prolific Nemirovsky is forever churning out. The charity of this artisan allows me to keep and use the furniture until it is sold. Just now I sleep inside a would-be Sung Dynasty vase, since an overstock of double beds has displaced me from my bedroom and a single folding throne denies me my dining room.

"I have dared include myself in the honorable circle of Deán Funes Street, since Madame Hsin indirectly encouraged me to ignore the justified curses of the others and from time to time to step across her threshold. This incomprehensible indulgence did not obtain the unconditional support of Tai An, who night and day was Madame Hsin's tutor, her master in magic. But my ephemeral paradise did not last as long as the years of the tortoise or the toad. Loyal to the magician's interests, Madame Hsin devoted herself to pleasing Nemirovsky so as to make his happiness complete and at the same time to make the quantity of furniture he produced exceed the permutations of one person seated at a number of tables. Fighting off nausea and boredom, she unselfishly endured the proximity of that bearded Western face, although, to make her martyrdom more bearable, she preferred seeing him in the dark or in the Loria movie house.

"This noble routine linked the furniture factory forever to the centipede of commercial prosperity. Renouncing his acquisitive nature, Nemirovsky spent on rings and fox furs the banknotes that now made his wallet fat as a pig. At the risk of being branded repetitive by some viperous critic, he piled these gifts on Madame Hsin's fingers and neck.

"Mr. Parodi, before continuing allow me an obvious clarification. Only a man whose head has been struck off could have imagined that these painful, usually evening, activities would come between Tai An and his shapely disciple. I admit to my illustrious contradictors that the lady did not stand rigid as an axiom in the magician's house. When her own face was unable to watch over and serve him, since several city blocks lay between them, she delegated these tasks to another face and a most inferior one—the face I humbly hold aloft, the face that now greets you and smiles.* I performed this delicate mission with genuine servility. So as not to bother the magician, I tried to moderate my presence; so as not to bore him, I changed costumes. Sometimes, hanging from a coathanger, I pretended with scant success to be the woolen overcoat that hid me. Other times, hastily disguised as a piece of furniture, I would appear in the corridor on all fours with a vase of flowers on my back. Unfortunately, an old monkey does not climb a rotten pole. Tai An, a cabinetmaker after all, recognized me only moments before unleashing a kick that forced me to impersonate other inanimate objects.

"But the Celestial Vault is more envious than the man who has just found out that one of his neighbors has acquired a sandalwood crutch and another a marble eye. Even the moment we observe a single sesame seed is not eternal, for so much happiness must come

*In fact, the doctor smiled and gave a greeting. [Author's note.]

to an end. The seventh of October brought us the conflagration that threatened Fang She's personal anatomy, broke up forever our little circle, burned down the house imperfectly, and devoured an inestimable number of wooden lamps. Do not dig in search of water, Mr. Parodi; do not dehydrate your honorable organism. The fire was put out. Alas, the instructive warmth of our circle has also been put out. Madame Hsin and Tai An moved by automobile to Cerrito Street. Nemirovsky used the insurance money to found a fireworks business. Fang She, quiet as an endless succession of identical teapots, remained in the wooden shed beside the lone willow tree.

"I did not betray any of the thirty-nine supplementary articles of truth when I admitted that the fire had been quenched, but only a priceless vessel of water could boast of quenching its memory. From early dawn, Nemirovsky and the magician were busy making fragile bamboo lamps of an indefinite and perhaps infinite number. Considering without bias the smallness of my house and the uninterrupted flow of furniture, I began to think that the artisans' vigil was pointless and that some of these lamps would never be lit. My goodness, before the night was out I had to admit my error. At eleven-fifteen P.M., all the lamps were burning, together with the bin of shavings and a wooden grille whose surface was painted green. The brave man is not he who treads on a tiger's tail but he who lies in ambush for it in the jungle, waiting for the moment preordained from the beginning of the universe to spring out in deadly assault. That is what I did. I persevered by climbing into the willow, ready as a salamander to leap into the fire at the first soft cry from Madame Hsin. It is well said that a fish on a roof sees better than a pair of eagles on the floor of the sea.

Without claiming to dub myself with the title of fish, I saw many distressing sights, but I endured them without falling, sustained by the pleasant prospect of reporting them scientifically to you. I saw the thirst and the hunger of the fire. I saw Nemirovsky, his face distorted by horror, trying to appease the fire with offerings of sawdust and newsprint. I saw the ceremonious Madame Hsin, who was following the magician's every move the way happiness follows rockets. Finally I saw the magician, who, after helping Nemirovsky, ran to the back shed and saved Fang She, whose happiness that night was frustrated on account of his hay fever. This rescue is all the more marvelous if we list its twenty-eight outstanding details, of which, with miserly brevity, I shall give only four.

"(a) The discredited fever which accelerated Fang She's pulse was not sufficiently outstanding to immobilize him in bed and prevent his elegant flight.

"(b) The colorless person who is now grunting out this account was perched in the willow tree, ready to flee with Fang She if the conflagration made it advisable.

"(c) The total immolation of Fang She would not have hurt Tai An, who fed and housed him.

"(d) As in man's body the tooth does not see, the eye not scratch, and the toenail not chew, so in the body which by convention we call a nation it is not proper that one individual usurp the role of another. The emperor does not abuse his position to sweep streets. The prisoner does not compete with the vagabond and wander about all over the place. In rescuing Fang She, Tai An usurped the role of the firemen at the grave risk of offending them and of being soaked by their copious hoses.

"It is well said that after the lawsuit is lost the hangman must be paid. After the fire, the dispute began. The magician and the cabinetmaker fell out. In immortal monosyllables General Su Wu has celebrated the pleasure of contemplating a bear hunt, but everyone knows he was shot in the back by the arrows of his own infallible bowmen and then overtaken and devoured by his angry prey. This imperfect analogy also fits Madame Hsin, who, like the general, was caught between two forces. She tried in vain to reconcile the two friends and, like a goddess who watches over the ruins of her temple, kept running from Tai An's charred bedroom to Nemirovsky's now limitless office. The *Book of Changes* notes that to please an angry man it is pointless to fire rockets and parade large numbers of floats. Madame Hsin's pleas and coaxings did not resolve the incomprehensible dispute; they may even have rekindled it. This situation drew on the map of Buenos Aires an interesting shape not unlike that of a triangle. Tai An and Madame Hsin honored an apartment on Cerrito Street with their presence. Nemirovsky, with his fireworks business, enjoyed bright new horizons at number 95 Catamarca Street. Fang She remained constantly in the shed.

"If the artisan and magician had heeded that triangle, I should not now be indulging in the undeserved pleasure of talking to you two. Unfortunately, Nemirovsky did not want to let Columbus Day go by without paying a visit to his old colleague. When the police arrived an ambulance had to be called. The mental balance of the opponents was so upset that Nemirovsky, paying no attention to an interminable nosebleed, intoned didactive verses from the Tao Te Ching, while the magician, unmindful of the loss of one of his upper canines, cracked an endless series of Jewish jokes.

149

"Madame Hsin was so grieved over their falling out that she frankly banned me from the door of her house. The adage says that the beggar expelled from the kennel takes up residence in the palace of memory. To outwit my loneliness I made a pilgrimage to the ruins on Deán Funes Street. Behind the willow the afternoon sun went down as in my diligent boyhood. Fang She received me with resignation and offered me a cup of plain tea, pine nuts, walnuts, and vinegar. The ubiquitous and solid figure of Madame Hsin did not prevent me from noticing an enormous steamer trunk which looked like a venerable ancestor in a state of putrefaction. Betrayed by the trunk, Fang She confessed to me that fourteen years spent in this paradise of a country hardly equaled a single minute of the most unbearable torture, and that he had already got from our consul a rectangular cardboard ticket home on the *Yellow Fish,* which sailed for Shanghai the following week. The garish dragon of his joy betrayed a single defect—the certainty of thwarting Tai An. In fact, if to assess the value of a priceless mink coat trimmed with sealskin the greatest expert takes into account the number of moths that dwell therein, so too a man's loneliness is assessed by the exact number of beggars who feed off him. Fang She's emigration would doubtless undermine Tai An's solid credit. To prevent that, Tai An was not beyond resorting to locks and watchmen, knots and drugs. Fang She countered these arguments with an amiable languor and begged me by all my maternal ancestors not to burden Tai An with the insignificant news of his departure. As the *Books of Rites* demands, I added the dubious guarantee of my paternal lineage, and the two of us embraced under the willow, not without a tear or two.

"Minutes later a taxicab deposited me on Cerrito Street. Undeterred by the imprecations of the butler, who was a mere tool of Madame Hsin and Tai An, I took cover in the corner drugstore. In this venal institution they attended to my eye and lent me a telephone. I dialed. As Madame Hsin did not answer, I confided to Tai An himself that his protégé proposed to flee. My reward was an eloquent silence, which lasted until I was thrown out of the pharmacy.

"It is well said that the fleet-footed postman who hastens to deliver his mail is more worthy of praise and dithyrambs than his colleague who drowses beside a fire fueled with the same mail. Tai An reacted quickly and efficiently. To nip in the bud his protégé's escape, he hastened to Deán Funes Street as if the stars had endowed him with more than one foot and more than one oar. At the house, two surprises awaited him. The first was to find Fang She out; the second was to find Nemirovsky in. Nemirovsky told him that some local merchants had seen Fang She load himself and a trunk onto a horse-drawn cart and disappear northward at a leisurely pace. In vain the two men searched for him. Then they took leave of each other, Tai An to go off to a furniture auction on Maipú Street and Nemirovsky to meet me at the Western Bar."

"Halte lá!" Montenegro ejaculated. "The drunkard rides roughshod over the artist. Look at the picture, Parodi. The duelists gravely lay down their weapons, touched in some common chord by the loss they both feel. I emphasize a strange thing. The cause that motivates them is one and the same, but the characters are fiercely dissimilar. Dismal premonitions probably fan Tai An's brow. He seeks, he interrogates, he asks questions. I confess that it's the third character who

intrigues me. This *jemenfoutiste* who rides away from the action of our story in an open car is a fascinating mystery."

"Gentlemen," continued Dr. Shu T'ung mildly, "my laborious narrative has reached the memorable night of October fourteenth. I take the liberty of calling it memorable because my uncivil, old-fashioned stomach could not appreciate the double helping of mush which was the ornament and only dish of Nemirovsky's table. My innocent aim had been: (a) to dine at Nemirovsky's; (b) to go to the Once Cinema and judge three musicals which, according to Nemirovsky, had not satisfied Madame Hsin; (c) to savor an anise liqueur at La Perla café; (d) to return home. The all too vivid and painful evocation of the mush forced me to give up items *b* and *c* and to subvert the natural order of your reputable alphabet, skipping from *a* to *d*. A secondary result was that I did not leave home all night in spite of insomnia."

"These remarks do you credit," said Montenegro. "Although our childhood's dishes are, in their way, priceless *trouvailles* of our Argentine heritage, I warmly agree with Dr. Shu T'ung. At the pinnacle of haute cuisine, the French chef admits no rival."

"On the fifteenth, two detectives personally awakened me," Shu T'ung continued, "and they invited me to keep them company to police headquarters. There I found out what you two already know. A little before daybreak the affectionate Nemirovsky, uneasy about Fang She's sudden mobility, had entered the house on Deán Funes Street. It is well said in the *Book of Rites* that if your honorable concubine cohabits in blazing summer with persons of low rank, one of your children will be a bastard. If you abuse your friends' palaces outside the established hours, an enigmatic smile will beautify the porters' faces. Nemirovsky felt in his own flesh the sting of this adage. He not only did not find Fang She, but instead came upon the magician's body, half buried under the willow tree."

"Perspective, my worthy Parodi, is the Achilles' heel of all great Oriental painters," Montenegro suddenly pontificated. "Between two blue mouthfuls of smoke, I will enhance the album of your mind with a swift *raccourci* of the scene. On Tai An's shoulder, death's haughty kiss had left the mark of its lipstick—a knife wound some four inches wide. Of the guilty weapon, not a trace. Someone had vainly attempted to make up for this missing clue with the burial spade, the commonest of garden tools, relegated, quite rightly, to a position a few yards away. On the rough handle of this tool, the police (incapable of any flight of imagination and sticklers for detail) have found some of Nemirovsky's fingerprints. The savant, the intuitive mind, laughs at this cooked-up scientific nonsense. It is the role of such a mind to build up, piece by piece, an enduring, elegant edifice. Let me slow down. I shall hold off until tomorrow the moment for revealing and engraving my insights."

"Always assuming your morrow will dawn," broke in Shu T'ung. "Let me again perpetrate my humble story. Tai An's safe entry into the house on Deán Funes Street went unnoticed by the unobservant neighbors, who slumbered like a shelf of classics in a library. It is thought, however, that he must have come in after eleven, because at a quarter to he was seen poking about the inexhaustible auction room on Maipú Street."

"I corroborate that fact," said Montenegro. "Let me whisper to you, *inter nos,* that the Buenos Aires grapevine reported the fleeting appearance of an exotic character. So here are the positions of the pieces on the board. At around eleven P.M., the queen—and I refer to Madame Hsin—shows her slanted eyes and shapely figure in the midst of the multicolored hubbub of the Bewildered Dragon. Between eleven and twelve she received at home a client who remains anonymous. *Le coeur à des raisons.* As to the shifty Fang She, the police claim that before eleven o'clock he took lodgings in the renowned 'old drawing room,' or 'millionaires' room,' at the New Impartial Hotel, an undesirable warren in our slum district, about which neither you nor I, my dear *confrère,* know a thing. On the fifteenth of October, he sailed on the *Yellow Fish,* bound for the mystery and glamour of the East. He was arrested in Montevideo, and he now vegetates inconspicuously here in Moreno Street at the disposal of the authorities. 'And what about Tai An?' the skeptic might ask. Deaf to the frivolous curiosity of the police, hermetically sealed in a typically bright-colored coffin, he rows and rows in the quiet hold of the *Yellow Sunset,* bound on his eternal voyage for ancient, ritualistic China."

II

Four months later, Fang She came to visit Isidro Parodi. He was a tall, flabby man. His face was round, empty, and somewhat mysterious. He wore a black straw hat and a white trench coat.

"Just in time," said Parodi.* "If you've nothing

*The duelists have crossed swords. The reader can already hear the clash of rival steel. [Marginal note by Gervasio Montenegro.]

against it, let me tell you what I know and what I don't know about the Deán Funes Street affair. Your fellow-countryman, Dr. Shu T'ung, who isn't here, gave us a long, confused account of it. From what he said I understand that in 1922 some blasphemer or other stole a relic from a statue of miraculous powers that you Chinese worship in your country. The priests were horror-struck at the news and sent a missionary to punish the heretic and to recover the relic. The doctor revealed that Tai An, on his own avowal, was the man sent on the mission. But let me stick to the facts, wise Merlin would say. The missionary Tai An kept changing his name and address. From the newspapers he knew about every ship that arrived in Buenos Aires, and he kept a watch on every Chinaman who disembarked. A person behaving in this way might be looking for something, or, equally, trying to hide. You reached Buenos Aires first; Tai An came later. Anyone would have thought that you were the thief and he the pursuer. But Dr. Shu T'ung himself said that Tai An had already been in Uruguay for a year trying to sell wafers. So, as you see, the first to arrive in South America was Tai An.

"Look, let me tell you what I've figured out. If I'm mistaken, please say, 'You're off the track, brother,' and put me right. I take it for granted that Tai An is the thief and you the missionary, otherwise the whole thing makes no sense.

"For a long time, Fang She, my friend, Tai An had been giving you the slip. That's why he kept changing his name and address. In the end, he got tired. He thought up a plan that was so bold it was foolproof, and he had the determination and the guts to carry it out. He started with a daring act. He made you go and live in his house. That was where the Chinese lady, who was his mistress, and the Jewish cabinetmaker lived. The lady was after the jewel, too. Every time she went out with the Jew, who also had a thing going with her, she left the doctor behind as her spy. The fellow was so resourceful that when necessary he'd put a flowerpot on his behind and become a piece of furniture in disguise. Spending so much on movie tickets and other things left the Jew without a cent. He pulled the old, old number and set fire to the furniture shop to collect the insurance money. Tai An was in cahoots with him. He helped him make the lamps that served as kindling for the blaze, and then the doctor, who was clinging as tightly to the willow as a salamander, caught the two helping the fire along with old newspapers and sawdust. Now let's see what everyone did during the fire. The lady followed Tai An like a shadow, waiting for the moment he'd take the jewel from its hiding place. But Tai An wasn't particularly concerned about the jewel. Instead, he saves you. This move can be looked at in two ways. One is to think you're the thief and they save you so the secret doesn't die with you. But as I see it, Tai An did what he did to stop you from pursuing him—to buy you off morally, if I make myself clear."

"That's so," Fang She said simply. "But I did not let myself be bought off."

"The first idea didn't satisfy me," Parodi went on. "Had you been the thief, who was it who feared you'd die with the secret? Besides, if there had been any real danger the doctor would have arrived on the scene like a telegram, flowerpot and all.

"The next day everyone went off, leaving you behind lonelier than one glass eye. Tai An pretended to fall out with Nemirovsky. I see two reasons for this. The first was to make everyone believe that he wasn't in cahoots with the Jew and that he deplored the fire. The second was to take the lady away, thus parting her from the Jew. A short time later, the Jew started taking her out again, and then he and Tai An began fighting in earnest.

"You were in a tight corner. The talisman might have been hidden anywhere. At first glance, one place seemed beyond suspicion—the house. There were three reasons for disregarding it. One, you were living there. Two, that's where they left you living alone after the fire. And three, Tai An had set fire to it himself. Still, I expect that Tai An went a bit too far. In your shoes, don Pancho, I would have been suspicious of all that proof to demonstrate something that didn't need demonstrating."

Fang She got to his feet and said gravely, "What you have said is true, but there are some things you can't possibly know. Let me tell you what they are. After everyone left, I was convinced that the talisman was hidden in the house. I didn't look for it. I asked our Chinese consul to repatriate me, and I confided the news of my journey to Dr. Shu T'ung, who, as one might have expected, immediately told Tai An. I left, put my trunk aboard the *Yellow Fish,* and returned to the house. I entered through the empty lot out back and hid. Sometime later, Nemirovsky arrived. The neighbors told him about my departure. Then Tai An arrived. Together they pretended to be looking for me. Tai An said he had to go to a furniture auction on Maipú Street. Each went his own way. Tai An had lied. A minute or two later he was back. He went into the shed and came out with the spade that I myself had so often used in the garden.* There in the moonlight, he

*A bucolic touch. [Original note by José Formento.]

began digging beside the willow. I'm not sure how much time passed. He unearthed something shiny, and at last I saw the goddess's talisman. I threw myself onto the thief and carried out the necessary punishment.

"I knew I'd be arrested sooner or later. But I had to save the talisman. I hid it in the dead man's mouth. Now the jewel is on its way home, on its way back to the shrine of the goddess, where my compatriots will find it when they cremate the body. After that I looked up the day's auction sales in a newspaper. There were two or three furniture auctions on Maipú Street. I looked in on one of them. At five minutes to eleven, I was already at the New Impartial Hotel. That's my story. Now you can hand me over to the authorities."

"Not a chance," said Parodi. "People nowadays expect the government to do everything for them. If you're poor the government has to find you a job. If you fall ill the government has to pay your hospital bill. Kill someone and instead of paying for it yourself you ask the government to punish you. You may say that I'm a fine one to talk like this, since the state is keeping me. But I still believe, sir, that a man has to shift for himself."

"I too believe that, Mr. Parodi," Fang She said deliberately. "Many men are dying in the world today in defense of that belief."

Pujato,
October 21, 1942

H. Bustos Domecq

We transcribe below a biographical outline by the schoolteacher Miss Adelma Badoglio:

Dr. Honorio Bustos Domecq was born in the hamlet of Pujato, in the province of Santa Fe, in the year 1893. After an interesting primary-school education, he moved with his family to the Chicago section of Buenos Aires. In 1907, the newspaper columns of Rosario accepted the early writings of this modest friend of the Muses without suspecting his age. The following compositions date from that period: "Vanitas," "The March of Progress," "Our Homeland, Blue and White," "To Her," "Nocturnes." In 1915, he read his "Ode to the 'Elegy on the Death of His Father' by Jorge Manrique" before a select audience at the Majorcan Club, an achievement which won him noisy but ephemeral fame. That same year he published *Citizen!*, a work of sustained imagination marred, unfortunately, by certain Gallicisms which may be blamed on the author's youth and the shortsightedness of the times. In 1919, he wrote *Fata Morgana,* a slim volume of occasional verse whose final stanzas herald the lively prose stylist of *Let's Speak Properly!* (1932) and *Among Books and Papers* (1934). During the Labruna government, he was first appointed Inspector of Schools and later Counsel for the Destitute. Away from the comforts of home, contact with harsh reality provided him with that experience which may be the principal source of his work. Among his books, let us list these: *The Eucharistic Congress, an Argentine Organ for the Propagation of the Faith; The Life and Death of Don Chicho Grande; Now I Can Read!* (by appointment of the City of Rosario School Board); *The Contribution of Santa Fe to the War of Independence;* and *New Stars: Azorín, Gabriel Miró, Bontempelli.* His detective stories reveal a new vein in this many-faceted, prolific writer. In them, he attempts to combat the cold intellectualism in which Sir Arthur Conan Doyle, Ottolenghi, etc., have immersed this genre. *Tales of Pujato,* as the author affectionately calls them, are not the filigree of a Byzantine locked in an ivory tower but are the voice of a true contemporary, who is sensitive to the human pulsebeat and from whose generous pen flows the torrent of his truths.